Accident Prone

Essa Sims

Published by Essa Sims, 2025.

ACCIDENT PRONE

First edition. January 27, 2025.

Copyright © 2025 Essa Sims.

ISBN: 979-8230547679

Written by Essa Sims.

Also by Essa Sims

Dark Adversary
Accident Prone

Chapter One

Jenny rubbed her hands over her sore eyes and yawned. *That's it! I've had enough.* She sighed tiredly, then sat back and studied the designs in front of her with a critical eye. Not bad, yet not good either, and trying to improve them in her present frame of mind was not conducive to producing anything better. She would continue tomorrow after having had a good night's sleep, and she could think with a clear mind.

Just a few years back when a student attending art college, Jenny had thought, in her innocence, that she would become a renowned artist. Gradually she had come to realise that her confidence had been misplaced, and she found that the world was a far more competitive place than first imagined when she had made such ambitious plans.

Jenny became disillusioned as time passed and jobs became scarce and had begun to explore different avenues in the art world. Finally, at the age of twenty-three, she had found her niche in designing wallpapers, her speciality being those she created for children, and her designs had gradually gained popularity in some of the smaller, yet exclusive design companies. Now a year later, she made an adequate amount of money to suit her needs. She enjoyed the work that she did and no longer had a burning ambition to do anything else. Yet this evening her creativity seemed to have deserted her entirely.

Jenny pushed her stool back and stood up stretching wearily. What she needed was to take a break and gain a different perspective on things. She heard the tinkle of the old shop bell; no matter how old she got, Jenny still loved that sound, and hastened through to serve what she hoped was the last customer of the day, glad of the distraction.

ןוןוןוןוןוןו

When the customer had gone, Jenny sighed with relief and locked the door. Not that she was about to complain about being so busy. All custom was welcome, but some days were more trying than others. This had been one such day. Now she would be glad to escape upstairs and have a good soak in the deep old-fashioned tub. It was a relic of the past they had inherited along with the old property, but at least she could lay full length in it and totally chill out.

Her hair, as usual, had gone its own unruly way and Jenny grimaced as she ran her fingers through the mass of long, wayward brown curls that framed her small face. Her pert nose and soft full mouth added to her overall appeal. Her best features were her large, heavily lashed green eyes. Her father's jewels, as he liked to call them. Jenny was a very lovely girl, a fact that she was unaware of. She acknowledged that she was attractive, yet because her sister Rachel was so elegant and beautiful, Jenny did not quite realise her own potential.

Rachel was taller than her, with delicate features and sparkling blue eyes. She had long wavy blonde hair that she usually wore up in a neat twist, and men tended to turn and stare as she passed, a fact that her sister was fully aware of and played upon. Rachel was a terrible flirt, yet her nature was such that most of her old boyfriends were still firm friends with her. Although their personalities were quite different, both sisters were fiercely protective of each other, especially where men were concerned.

ןוןוןוןוןוןו

Jenny and her sister ran a small shop in the tiny, picturesque Sussex village of Tyneham, which they stocked with all sorts of oddments from new to second-hand. Donations were always coming in and welcome. Old books, clothes, many from firms with an end-of-stock clearance, anything that might be of interest, and they had a surprising number of customers for such a small community. Somehow, they managed to make a living from the small income the shop provided, along with Jenny's earnings.

Rachel was waiting for a teaching post to come up, but in the meantime, she ran the shop and left her sister to get on with her wallpaper designs, although Jenny did take a turn occasionally just to give Rachel a break. Sometimes it came as a relief to stand and stretch, then walk about the shop after being hunched over her design table for too long.

Jenny's design area was at the back of the shop and the door opened out on to a small, paved square of garden, littered with pots of colourful flowers. In the summer, the sun streamed into the tiny workroom, lighting it up, making it a pleasure to relax in, and it was the girls' habit, if the weather was kind, to sit outside together each lunchtime at the old wooden garden table, and drink their coffee along with a light salad or sandwiches.

Above the shop was an artfully arranged flat, which could only be reached by way of a narrow gravel path that ran down the side of the property, this ended at a beautifully thatched porch that hung over the low front door. Both girls had fallen in love with the cottage at first sight and were determined to purchase it.

The whole place was oddly arranged. Someone in the past had decided to separate the flat above the shop from the workroom and display area below to obtain the utmost room. Their entry door, now at the side of the building near the gate to their back patio, opened into a small square hall, with the stairs directly facing them, and when reaching the top, a narrow door on the right led through to the flat. The only time this became a hindrance was when trying to move furniture in or in inclement weather, and they had become accustomed to always carrying an umbrella between their trips to and from the flat to the shop.

The living quarters and shop had come as a package, and with the proceeds that came with the sale of their parents' large house, they could well afford it, with some left over for security. Not that their parents were dead as most people assumed, but they in turn had inherited a beautiful old house in Scotland from the girls' maternal grandmother and decided to start anew, leaving their present home to Jenny and Rachel to do with as they chose. Their parents had never really settled in the house, it was too modern for their taste, but their father's job at the time had dictated where they were to dwell. Now they were living in their chosen habitat and were delighted that the girls were managing so well.

At first, Jenny and Rachel had felt guilty about accepting the house, but as their mother said, "Don't make me wait until I die before I can leave you something. Humour me and know that it makes us happy." So, they had sold the house, bought the shop, and now here they both were, missing their parents, but happily settled. The only blot on the horizon, as far as Jenny was concerned, was one Jason Hawkins.

He was an attractive man, tall, slim, with a ready smile and neatly trimmed fair hair. Jason was likeable and welcoming, but most definitely not her type. He ran a small art gallery in the nearby town and had decided, on seeing Jenny, that she was the girl of his dreams.

When the girls had first moved in, they were interested to hear from one of their customers that a small art gallery a few miles down the road had an exhibition due, and they decided to go and attend the first opening day.

"Free drinks and nibbles, Jen, what more could you ask?" said Rachel with enthusiasm, so they had duly visited the gallery and had thoroughly enjoyed themselves, until they had met Jason, who, to be fair, could not be faulted. He was charming and polite, yet immediately as he made his attraction to her clear, Jenny knew that she was going to have a problem.

At first, Jenny was flattered by the fact that Jason had flirted with her instead of Rachel, who usually drew any male attention. Now he was becoming a bit of a pain. She did everything to put him off, but the colder she acted toward him, the more his desire for her appeared to grow. Jenny had been right, and now she was beginning to run out of excuses, it was obviously time to be blunter.

Jenny shook her head at the thought of him, and as though she had conjured him up, there he was, tapping on the window. Her heart sank, but she nodded politely, wishing that Rachel hadn't chosen today to go into town and choose some new clothes. She peered at him through the glass, pointing at the closed sign, but he tapped again. Jenny sighed with annoyance and opened the door, pasting a polite smile on her face.

"What do you want, Jason? We're closed."

"What do you think I could possibly want in your little shop?" he scoffed, glancing around with a faint look of distaste. An attitude that did not go down too well with the girl looking up at him. Jason, completely unaware of how that scathing comment sounded, looked hopefully at her. "Jen, I wondered if you'd like to have dinner with me in town tonight?"

"Sorry, Jason," Jenny said shortly. "I am otherwise engaged."

"Perhaps another time," he asked anxiously, obviously put out by her less than welcoming attitude.

"I don't think that would be very wise, Jason." She held the door open pointedly.

"Why can't you at least have lunch with me?" Jason asked plaintively, stopping in the doorway.

"You are a very nice man, Jason, and I'm sure there are plenty of girls out there who would love to go out with you, just not me," Jenny said firmly, as she gave him a dismissive smile, ignoring the despairing look he gave.

"I won't give up, you know," Jason said, as he walked off despondently.

Jenny shut the door after him with a sense of relief. His persistence was becoming quite annoying, yet she could not help feeling sorry for him. He made her feel guilty, but pity was not a good enough reason to go out with the man. It would simply encourage him, adding to the problem, and she certainly did not want to give Jason any false hopes.

What she needed was to get away from all the pressure. A holiday was the answer. A place to unwind where she would have time and solitude to dream up some innovative designs. Somewhere quiet and tranquil.

ꝏ ꝏ ꝏ ꝏ ꝏ ꝏ

As she came out of the shop and locked the door behind her, Jenny paused and glanced across the road to the village green, smiling as she saw the ducks on the pond fighting over the crumbs being thrown to them by old Mrs Perrin. She could set her watch by the elderly woman's lunchtime visits to feed her feathered friends, as she called them.

Her gaze took in the sunlight sparkling on the water, and then she looked around at the fields beyond, with the small cottages half hidden in the lanes among the foliage of intersecting hedges. It was a beautiful view, and Jenny could hardly say that it was not tranquil here, but she still desperately needed a break from her daily routine.

The village boasted several shops, and somehow managed to keep them going, thanks to passing trade brought in by customers who drove through on their way to the pretty coastal towns beyond. It was so lovely here, and Jenny breathed in deeply, savouring the freshness of the air, then coughed as a particularly noisy car raced past throwing out a cloud of fumes. Unfortunately, that was happening all too often these days, and she felt sad at the thought of the village becoming spoilt by through traffic.

ꝏ ꝏ ꝏ ꝏ ꝏ ꝏ

Later that evening, Jenny sat snuggled in her bathrobe, sipping a warm drink as she spread the holiday brochures she had obtained from the local travel agent out onto the table. Rachel was out with her latest boyfriend and Jenny had the place to herself, so she could browse through the glossy pages without fear of interruption. She took her time, dismissing them one by one until her eye was caught by the word peaceful.

"Ah, now that sounds exactly what I'm looking for," Jenny murmured, as she read on. The hotel was in Devon and described as small, select, and remote, all the attributes that she was searching for. Added to its appeal was the fact that the building was placed right at the edge of the moors, and you could not get more isolated than that. Making sure that her sister had no objection to running the shop alone for a week, Jenny immediately made her travel arrangements.

ꙄꙄꙄꙄꙄꙄ

Jenny glanced up at Rachel who stood watching as she packed. "Are you sure that you'll be all right on your own running the shop, sis? I can always postpone this vacation until another time."

"For heaven's sake, stop worrying about me, Jen. I can cope perfectly well." Her sister rolled her eyes. "I am only three years younger than you, not ten, now go and enjoy yourself! Apart from producing more brilliant designs, you might meet the man of your dreams."

"Huh! Chance would be a fine thing," Jenny snorted. "Dream man says it all. The only place they exist is in our dreams! I have yet to meet a live one who lights my fire."

"Don't be such a grouch," Rachel laughed.

Jenny smiled in amusement. "Now you have firsthand evidence of why I need time off."

"Just go enjoy yourself, Jen," her sister smiled back.

Chapter Two

J enny felt herself beginning to unwind as the train took her farther and farther away from her problems, not that they were many and would have to be faced again when she returned, but for now she was determined to relax and have a good time. When she duly arrived at her destination, Jenny was thrilled to see that the hotel was a dreamy old, thatched building, with a pretty vine mingling with roses growing up past the front windows and around the door. Picture perfect. So far so good!

She stood and drank in the beauty of the scene, feeling her tension begin to drain away. How long was it since she had done something this simple, just stood and appreciated the peace and comforting ambience of the countryside, without giving a thought to anything else?

This place more than lived up to the description given, because this hotel was certainly remote, Jenny thought, as she gazed around at the rolling hills and fields that surrounded the building. Towering over everything stood the tors, beckoning to be explored. She smiled with anticipation as she stared up at them, then picked her case up and walked inside the hotel.

That night Jenny slept like a top, and the next morning when she flung the curtains wide, she was filled with a wonderful sense of wellbeing.

"What a beautiful morning! A walk beckons," she murmured happily. Breathing in that fresh unpolluted air should certainly get her creative juices flowing. First, she needed to go down to the dining room and eat a hearty breakfast, before setting out on her trek up to the tors. She must also remember to take a bottle of water with her. The steep and rocky terrain, as the manager informed her, was guaranteed to bring on a thirst.

Jenny muffled up, because although it was only still late summer, she knew that the wind up on the moors could be quite chilly at times.

୪୪୪୪୪୪

As she left her room and turned to lock the door behind her, a body suddenly collided violently with hers and muscular arms wrapped firmly around her. She gasped in shock as her wits temporarily deserted her, then found her voice as the arms tightened.

"What are you...? Get off me!" Jenny shrieked, half turning and as she did so, could see that the man had no shirt on. Her eyes widened in a mixture of growing fear and outrage, as she tried to break free, but his arms clamped even more firmly around her body. "Oh! Right, one of those are you?" she yelled, enraged. She was in attack mode and prepared to defend herself to the death. Slipping one arm free and pulling it back, Jenny clenched her fist, then thumped him squarely on the nose with all the force she could muster.

An agonised groan greeted the impact and the man's arms immediately relinquished their hold, as he frantically clamped both hands to his face. Blood gushed between his fingers and dripped down onto the front of her dress and coat, then he dropped to his knees. As he happened to be still leaning against her at the time, she also went down, landing in an ungainly heap beneath him. Jenny tried to wriggle free and get up, but her foot slipped on some of the droplets of blood spattered across the floor.

As she jerked her leg up to gain a foothold, her knee connected painfully with his groin, and Jenny was amazed at the speed with which his hands transferred their grip. Then he slowly toppled forward as the air whooshed out of him, until his face was pressed against her stomach, which of course was when one of the other guests came upon them.

The woman let out a cry of horror at the sight that greeted her. The young lady in front of her was lying spread-eagled on the landing floor, with a man clamped between her legs. Not only was he in a very compromising position, but the man was also stark naked and moaning.

She set about him with her thick magazine, she might not be young, the woman thought, but she could still inflict some damage.

"Get off, you pervert! Help! Help," she screamed at the top of her lungs, beating at his hunched body with the rolled-up magazine.

When he turned his head and looked dazedly at her, the woman screamed even louder, because his face was covered in blood. It was only now that Jenny had collected her wits, she was able to get a good look at her assailant and become aware with horrified fascination that he was totally naked.

"My God! You're naked. She's right, you are a pervert," she stuttered, trying madly to scramble backwards. It was like trying to climb out from under a fallen tree, because she was pinned by him against her own door.

Jenny thought she heard him mutter something like. "Let me die, this just has to be a bad dream."

By now to add to the confusion, the manager had come galloping up the stairs, followed closely by some of the staff and a few other guests, curious as to what the ruckus was all about. Jenny was studying her assailant's face, and quickly realised that the man was totally confused and appalled by the situation he now found himself in.

"What's your room number?" she hissed into his ear, trying to penetrate his agonised daze. She had to repeat it several times before he could hear her question over his noisy gasps, but he couldn't speak. This was getting her nowhere and Jenny was becoming extremely conscious of his large body resting upon hers, his heavy dark head pressing down on her chest. Jenny smiled feebly up at the elderly woman, noticing with growing embarrassment that quite a few interested spectators had now gathered.

"I don't think that he's fully aware of exactly what's happening," Jenny said to the curious onlookers milling around them. She glanced back at the man's agonised expression, and her eyes began to catalogue the bulging muscles pressed so closely against her. He was gorgeous, or would be if his nose wasn't so swollen, and his face twisted in a grimace. Jenny blushed, as her eyes travelled down his body, and for some reason, her gaze became fascinated by the play of light on his tanned skin, and it was with great reluctance that she dragged her eyes away and back to the woman bending over her.

"We had an unfortunate encounter, that's all, and he appears to be quite confused," Jenny said to her. "I don't think he was attacking me, only reaching out for help."

The woman's lips twitched, as her eyes wandered over the powerful body of the man, still doubled up on top of the young woman. Her eyes caught Jenny's, and they exchanged a faint smile. He was a large man in every way, that was obvious. Jenny pulled herself together, flushing at her own thoughts. What on earth is wrong with me? Jenny wondered, as she looked up at her audience. This was more than embarrassing, it was horrific, and certainly not the right time to be assessing his looks. Although she had to acknowledge that he was quite an impressive looking specimen. Easy on the eye as her mother was apt to say.

ꖌ ꖌ ꖌ ꖌ ꖌ ꖌ

As the manager leaned down to pull the man off her, a tall, elegant woman came hurriedly along the corridor towards them, holding a man's dressing gown out in front of her.

"Oh, darling! Are you all right?" she said, bending over the man, while at the same time hastily trying to cover his body with the robe. She managed to get one of his arms in, and with the manager's help, slipped it over the other and quickly tied the belt, with the manager and another member of the staff supporting his weight. The woman blushed as she looked around at all the watching faces.

"I am so sorry, everyone. He sometimes sleepwalks if he's in a strange place, and I usually lock the door, but I had just slipped down to reception for a moment."

The woman heaved an apologetic sigh, as she looked down with concern at Jenny. "Oh, heavens! Look at your clothes, they are absolutely ruined. All that blood won't easily be removed."

Jenny looked down at herself and recoiled. She was spattered with blood stains and must look like something out of a horror movie to the other guests.

"At least I'm not hurt."

The other woman's eyes darted to the man's face in growing concern. His nose looked twice the size it should be, and the way he was clutching at his body, made it obvious that his nose was the least of his problems. She glanced back at Jenny and indicated the manager. "Please let Malcolm take care of everything, and of course, I shall pay for this unfortunate mess. Sorry once again." She took the man's arm, talking quietly to him. He was still bent double, as she helped him to his feet and supported him, as he hobbled painfully away to his room.

The manager was now apologising profusely to Jenny, offering to send her clothes to be cleaned, and his eyes twinkled with humour as he watched the retreating man. "I think he came off worse from the encounter, don't you?" he said, glancing down at her with a slight smile.

"That's debatable," Jenny replied, looking down at her rumpled and stained clothing wryly. She had not done her coat up, waiting until going down into the lobby, which meant her dress had caught its share of blood spatters and was badly stained. "At least I'm not the one in pain. All I sustained was a bump on the head as I slid down the door."

The manager immediately looked concerned, giving a faint frown as he studied the bump on her forehead. "Are you quite sure that you will be all right?"

Thanking him for his concern and assuring him that there was no cause for worry, Jenny let herself back into the sanctuary of her room and closed the door firmly behind her. Her head did ache, as it happened, but nothing a good rest wouldn't cure, and she had a feeling that she would find a few bruises on her back from hitting the floor. Finding herself beneath his heavy body had not helped. She could feel the heat suffusing her face at the mere thought and hurriedly rushed into the bathroom to tear off her clothes and splash her face with cold water. It didn't help to alleviate her embarrassment at what had just occurred, and the thought of facing the other guests at mealtimes was out of the question. Room service only.

If Jenny could have seen ahead, she would have packed and left immediately. As it was, she spent the rest of the day hiding, hoping the other guests would soon forget the unfortunate encounter. Some holiday this is, Jenny thought, day one and already something has gone wrong.

ॼ ॼ ॼ ॼ ॼ ॼ

The next day the lure of the moors that Jenny could see from her window could not be denied, so she decided to go out and fill her lungs with some fresh air. Before she left her room, Jenny cautiously put her head out and peered left and right furtively. No sign of a naked man. In fact, no sight of anyone. I mean, how many naked men could one encounter in such a brief space of time? Jenny gave an amused giggle. Good, now to get things back on an even keel. This was the start of her holiday, and she was going to make the most of it.

It was beautiful up on the moors and she threw her head back, letting the wind blow through her hair, tangling it into unruly curls. Jenny felt invigorated and she laughed aloud happily. This was just what she had needed to stimulate her creative juices, and Jenny drank in the fresh air greedily, closing her eyes, listening to her own soft breathing and the muted sound of sheep and birds. No sound of human voices to disturb the air. Pure bliss.

Jenny could also hear water gurgling somewhere nearby. Behind that interesting low outcrop of boulders perhaps? She would investigate the source later. Now, which way to go from here? The track Jenny was presently standing on was wide, with the hill sloping upwards on one side and falling away into a gently rolling slope on the other down to the lower ground. Obvious answer. Walk up towards the tors. They were the ancient rock formations she had wanted to visit, and now she could look at them closely, touch the weather-worn stone and imagine all the people over time who had laid their hands directly on the very same patch.

Unfortunately, Jenny was enjoying herself so much that she had not noticed how the overhanging branches of a small copse of trees on a bend in the track were obscuring her approach from the two walkers coming in the opposite direction. Jenny twirled happily, then came to an abrupt stop, nearly choking as her long scarf flew out and became snagged on the base of a thorny shrub on the opposite side of the path.

She hastily unwound it from her neck, lowering it and moving forward, then Jenny pulled it hard, but it stayed stubbornly attached. "Darn it," she muttered, as she took another two steps back and tugged it again, stretching it taut. Then to her utter disbelief, right at that moment a couple suddenly appeared and the man's leg became entangled with the scarf, and as he pulled it free, with a frantic shout of alarm he catapulted over the edge of the hill.

She rushed over in time to see him perform a spectacular cartwheel before he thudded to the ground below, rolling through a stagnant pool on his way down. Jenny now knew where the sound of water was coming from. The man had stopped short of a cascading torrent of water, not very deep, fortunately, because one side of his body was partially submerged in the icy cold stream. Jenny put her hands over her mouth to stop the nervous laugh, which was choosing this inappropriate time to escape. He had only fallen a short way, and the drop was not that steep, so he couldn't have sustained any major damage. Even so, she was trembling with dismay and apprehension.

The man lay still for a moment, then dragged himself away from the water, his sodden clothes dripping uncomfortably as he struggled to get to his hands and knees. Jenny could hear his laboured breathing even from where she was standing. Her eyes widened as he lifted his head. Oh, God, it was him! Did fate have it in for her? She must have done something terrible to deserve such bad luck.

She glanced guiltily sideways at the woman who had now joined her, and drew her breath in. It was the same woman who had been with the man yesterday, and she was gazing down at Jenny's unfortunate victim with a mesmerised expression.

"Sorry, so sorry," Jenny stammered, feeling even more guilty. "I hope he hasn't hurt himself too badly?"

"Darling, tell me that you are all right," the woman called down to him.

"I still appear to be in one piece... I think," the man gasped, looking up with glazed eyes. They suddenly narrowed as he spotted Jenny looking down at him, and he bellowed accusingly, "You!"

The woman had torn her eyes away from the dishevelled man and was staring at Jenny with renewed interest.

Jenny swallowed nervously. The gods were most definitely displeased with her.

ꑭ ꑭ ꑭ ꑭ ꑭ ꑭ

Jenny decided that now might be a suitable time to make a strategic retreat, and turned away, walking swiftly back down along the track towards the shortcut through the woods to the hotel. The woman called after her, but she rushed quickly on pretending not to hear and broke into a trot as she neared the trees. She wanted to get back well before they did and escape to the safety of her room. With any luck, she wouldn't even see them again.

"Well done, Jenny, your second day and look what happens. That poor man," she groaned to herself as she reached her room, then slammed and locked the door securely behind her. Jenny gave a groaning laugh at the memory of his sprawled body, then sobered and sighed. "I mustn't laugh. He could have been badly hurt."

Jenny did not dare leave her room again that day, so she phoned down for room service and spent the rest of the day and all evening catching up on the book that she had brought with her, not for one moment thinking that she would have had the chance to read it. If she went on at this rate she could join the local library. Hopefully, the rest of her stay should be uneventful.

Chapter Three

Another cloudless day dawned, and she got slowly out of bed, trying to decide how best to spend her time. Jenny decided it may be wiser if she left the vicinity of the hotel altogether and explored further afield.

It was a long walk down to the small town, but she thoroughly enjoyed it and spent the whole morning browsing around the shops. Not that there were many, but those she went in were interesting, especially the local gift shop. Her trip was spoilt by the fact that Jenny could not stop looking furtively around her all the time, in case she saw that darned man. Jenny's mind recalled his image, and she swallowed. He was incredibly good-looking, dark, and tall, very well built, and she speculated on his height. She had only seen him hunched in pain, but had he been standing straight, he must at least top six foot three or more. She blushed as her imagination conjured up his naked body. Why couldn't she remember him with clothes on, for heaven's sake? She gave a snort of laughter, making an old man standing nearby back away warily.

Jenny was tired, her feet ached, and she was hungry, so she decided to head back to the hotel and indulge herself with one of their delicious lunches. As she made her way back, the sun came out with a vengeance and Jenny began to flag. By the time she had reached the grounds of the hotel, she was even hotter and could feel the perspiration trickling down her forehead.

As she entered the doors of the hotel, an elderly lady in front of her stopped and appeared to be having trouble pushing the strong inner door open, so Jenny stepped forward politely and opened it for her. She held it with one hand as the lady thanked her profusely and passed through into the lobby.

"So kind, my dear. Not many left with such good manners," she said, with a grateful smile, and Jenny smiled back. At least she had done one thing right today. Perhaps the fates would relent? No such luck! As Jenny followed the woman through the door, she was aware of approaching footsteps behind her, so she tried to hold the door back, but her hand was moist and no matter how desperately she held on, it slipped off, allowing the door to slam shut. Jenny heard an agonised howl of pain and did not need to look behind her to know who was on the receiving end. Somehow the sound of his anguish was becoming all too familiar.

She threw a muffled apology in the general direction of the hunched body and this time she fled even quicker than before, haring up the stairs two at a time, before collapsing breathlessly back against her door. Jenny didn't know whether to laugh or cry. So much for lunch. She would have to give that a miss today. Once more room service was called into action and again, she sat with her book, wondering why all this was happening to her.

༒ ༒ ༒ ༒ ༒

The next day after her shower, Jenny wrapped herself in the cosy bathrobe provided, sat at the small table placed beneath the widow, and ate a leisurely breakfast, then rifled through the wardrobe for something smart to wear. She would catch the bus and go into one of the larger towns. Surely there was no way she could possibly bump into that man there?

Just as Jenny bent and laid her clothes out on the bed, there was a peremptory thump, and then the door flew open, and an irate figure appeared in the entrance.

"I would like a word with you, if you don't mind," an angry voice growled.

"Haven't you heard of knocking?" Jenny gasped, as she backed away. It was him again! The sight of him took her breath away. If she had thought him imposing before, now he was wearing a dark suit and looked spectacular. Hmm, handsome does not a nice man make, she decided, as she saw the grim set to his face.

"I did knock," the man stated impatiently.

"Well, I certainly did not hear you," Jenny said, shortly. "Thumping on someone's door and walking straight in is not knocking and waiting for an answer! I am sorry about what happened, I really am, but none of it was deliberate, and I did apologise. I don't know what else I can say. I mean, you started all this, and don't try and blame me for your sleepwalking habit, and how dare you come barging into my room and give me that accusing look, you bully?!"

The man looked as though he would like to choke her. He had never been accused of bullying in his life before. He paused, unless you considered his three brothers and sister, and... What am I doing? He felt enraged at his own distracted thoughts.

Jenny noticed that even though his hand was heavily bandaged, he still managed to clench it menacingly. "Get out of my room, I have no wish to talk to you anymore." She cleared her throat nervously and turned to escape into the bathroom. "I've apologised and that's all I can do, now please go."

"Not so fast," he roared, grabbing at the back of her robe.

As he did so, a voice from the doorway demanded. "What is going on here?"

The man stopped, but Jenny's impetus carried her forward, and he was left with the robe dangling from his outstretched hand. A tide of colour swept into his face, equally matching the colour in hers, as she saw his gaze fixed on her exposed breasts. Now it was her turn to stand almost naked. Thank goodness she was still wearing her panties. Maybe she would pass out and be spared from further humiliation.

Jenny closed her eyes, but nothing happened. She opened them again and blew her breath out on an embarrassed sigh.

The man's eyes seemed to glue themselves onto the small, slender body in front of him. They wandered down tracing a path over her shoulders, down to her beautiful small, but full breasts and slender waist. His heart rate increased, as he continued his exploration and slowed at the junction of her legs, moving on down the length of the long slender limbs. As the man became aware of what he was doing, he felt horrified and jerked his head up, meeting her large, shocked eyes, and the hot embarrassed flush that flooded her face as her hands frantically sought to cover herself. To her, the scene seemed to draw out far too long, when in reality it was only a matter of moments.

There was a dreadful silence, and as he tore his eyes away from her body, he muttered. "Okay! Now would be a good time for me to wake up." No, that excuse could not be used this time. He was wide awake and very aware of who had caused this situation. He hastily threw the robe towards Jenny and turned to face the two people framed in the doorway. One was the woman who had accompanied him before, the other was the manager, not looking quite so amused this time. He also had to wrench his eyes away from Jenny's slender form, before he confronted the two watching them.

The manager was the first to speak. "Would you care to explain what exactly you are doing in this young lady's bedroom? I think I am right in assuming that she did not invite you in, sir. Your raised voices disturbed some of the other guests and I really cannot tolerate this sort of behaviour in my hotel."

"Now, Malcolm, I'm sure there is a perfectly reasonable explanation, and I am as interested as you are in hearing it," the woman stated, as she put her hand on his arm to calm him. "This should be good. Darius?"

She faced them, waiting with arms folded and firmed her lips as she observed the tide of red that had swept the man's face, and the poor young woman looked absolutely mortified. Even though the girl was now securely wrapped in her dressing gown once again.

"It was just a misunderstanding, a private disagreement, really. A complete accident," he mumbled. It sounded feeble even to him and his voice faded away.

"Honestly, it was just one of those silly situations that arises," Jenny added, as she stepped towards the manager.

Her unwelcome visitor's head jerked towards her. "Not to me, they don't!" he rasped in exasperation. "Not until I had the misfortune to encounter you."

Jenny glared at him, incensed by his unfairness. He was the one who had started all this, and she was only trying to lighten the situation. She had not thrown her naked body at him and then blamed him for it. "How like a man," she snapped. "Nothing is ever your fault!"

"I'm glad you recognise that fact," he said with a smug, superior air that threatened to send her blood pressure soaring beyond the normal safety boundaries.

"You really are a pompous, swollen-headed moron," Jenny shouted, her voice rising and becoming shrill with outrage. She wanted to commit a violent act upon his body. His head was too far above her, so it was his midriff that she contemplated launching an attack on. She took a step toward him, her eyes flashing with anger.

"Calm down, you're becoming hysterical." The man stepped back in faint alarm as he saw the ferocious scowl on her face. Someone that small could not harm him, could they? He found his lips twitching at the very idea.

Jenny shut her eyes and breathed in deeply, trying to gain control of her temper, until he added with a mocking smile, "So, all these little incidents were accidental, were they? There are easier ways to attract my attention you know. Less painful anyway."

Her head threatened to burst as her rage reached epidemic proportions, and she bristled with indignation. "Attract you!" Jenny shrieked. "You have to be kidding, Mr. love-myself, and you have to be delusional to even think it! You must possess the mind of a slug, and the personality of a deathwatch beetle to even utter such twaddle! Why would anybody in their right mind want to attract you? Anybody would think you were someone of importance, which in my world you are most definitely not!"

He looked stunned, for once bereft of words as he gazed down at the quivering virago in front of him. A strange sound penetrated their war of words, and both faces turned as muffled laughter erupted from the doorway. Jenny was shocked to see the woman convulsed with mirth. She could not see what was so humorous about finding your boyfriend in another woman's room in what Jenny would have thought looked like a compromising situation. Humiliation washed over her, as she saw that even the manager was having a tough time trying to keep a straight face.

Jenny put her hands on her hips and lifted her chin pugnaciously. "I didn't invite any of you in, and I want you all to leave right now." She marched over, held the door wide, and pointed through it. "Now, if you don't mind."

The woman walked forward and grabbed the man's arm, managing to get him moving towards the door, looking back with amusement at the young woman's theatrical pose. Jenny was still standing rigidly, her body bristling with bottled-up anger and with her hand raised toward the corridor. She slammed it shut behind them, breathing hard.

Jenny did not know if she was horribly embarrassed, or just plain angry. Although angry was a tame word to describe the pulsating fury coursing through her quivering body. That's it, holiday thoroughly spoilt by that disagreeable man. She would apologise to the manager for her rudeness and check out first thing in the morning. Murder had not been on her agenda when Jenny had booked this holiday, but it might very well occur if she stayed.

ന ന ന ന ന ന

Outside on the landing, the woman, Gina, stood talking in a hushed voice to the manager, who listened with a half-smile, as she explained the situation, while Darius stalked ahead. Having smoothed everything over, Gina ran to catch up with her brother, who now had a face like thunder.

"She must have been out with a few slugs in her time to even know that they have a mind," he muttered savagely. "And what does she mean, the personality of a deathwatch beetle? What would she know?"

"Oh, come on, Darius, you had some nerve barging into that poor girl's room like that. Whatever were you thinking? No wonder she was so mad." His sister was still chuckling, as she followed him along the corridor. "The trouble is most girls usually fall at your feet, and you can't possibly imagine one who doesn't."

"Stop exaggerating, and I'm not that damned conceited," he growled, glaring down at her. "It's just that this isn't the first time I have been waylaid by a determined woman."

Gina was intrigued as she gazed up at her tall, handsome brother with amusement. This was the first time that she had seen him so undone by a woman. He was practically gnashing his teeth with anger. Her brother, who could normally manage women with such consummate ease. Darius hesitated and glared back down the corridor, as though he was contemplating having another set to with the girl.

"No, you don't!" Gina said sharply, pulling at his arm. "You have already caused enough of a ruckus here, so don't you dare start trouble off again. I've only just managed to convince the manager that you were only having a lover's tiff."

"What?!" he snarled, coming to an abrupt halt. "You have to be kidding, who would want to go out with a shrew like that?"

"Stop bellowing, Darius," Gina soothed, as she tried to push him along.

"I will make as much noise as I like," he roared. Then as though Darius had suddenly become aware of what he must look and sound like in her eyes, he made a concerted effort to quieten down, amazed at his own childish behaviour. "What the heck is the matter with me?" Darius rubbed his chin in disbelief. "I'm a grown man; these sorts of scenes just do not occur in my ordered existence."

Gina could not help laughing at his dumbstruck expression, and Darius threw his sister a furious and impatient glance as he strode away to his room ahead of his sister and slammed the door to stop her from following him. As Darius sat on his bed, he found his mind dwelling on the scene that had just taken place. If ever there was a case for exorcism, that girl was it! Failing that, they could pull the Witchfinder General out of retirement. It would be his moment of greatest glory.

Much to his disgust, Darius found that he could not get that darned woman out of his mind. She even invaded his dream that night, coming in through his window on a broomstick, where she spent the rest of the night searching for a cat that she insisted had been with her when she first entered. By the time morning came, Darius did not know which to strangle first, her or the cat.

ת ת ת ת ת ת

The next morning, Jenny frantically packed, fearful that the man would stage a repeat performance and come barging in again. She phoned for a taxi, pacing agitatedly about the room until she judged it was due to arrive. Jenny edged out of her room like a fugitive and flew down the stairs as if the devil were after her, standing outside half hidden behind a bush until the taxi made an appearance.

Jenny sniggered breathlessly to herself as the car carried her away from the scene of her undignified encounters with that beast of a man, then dropped her off at the station. As the train pulled away eating up the miles and placing distance between herself and the object of her humiliation, Jenny gradually began to relax back in her seat. If her friends could see her now, they would never believe it was the same person they knew so well. Finding oneself caught up in such a bizarre situation only happened in films, or so she had naively thought. She wanted to pinch herself at the sense of unreality she was experiencing. This was one holiday she could well have done without. The good thing was that she was nearing her destination leaving behind any further confrontations. As for a holiday, that would not be happening again for an extremely long time.

Chapter Four

When Jenny reached the haven of the flat, she sank down gratefully into a chair and kicked her shoes off, lying back with relief. Home at last. She let her heavy lids close, trying to erase that unpleasant man from her thoughts. Not that she would object to waking up and finding him in her Christmas stocking, just so long as he didn't open his mouth and speak. She sighed and gave a small laugh at her own silly thoughts and behaviour. What must they both have looked like to the two people watching them with such interest? Some holiday that had turned out to be.

Jenny had no recollection of ever losing her temper like that in the whole of her life. In fact, she was renowned for her calm and even temperament, yet that awful man had seemed to possess the capacity to reduce her to a gibbering maniac in the space of a few minutes. She chuckled as she remembered the look on his face when she had last seen him. It seemed she had the same effect upon him, because if looks could kill, she would be dead and buried under one of those tors by now. Someone in the future would stumble across her remains and wonder how she came to be planted under the heaviest stone, conclude she must be a witch, and decide to leave her trapped. Jenny laughed aloud at her own wandering imagination.

She experienced a sense of triumph as she recalled the dumbstruck look on the man's face when she had insulted him. Then she felt a twinge of embarrassment as she remembered how childish her words had sounded. Darius, the woman had called him. Nice name, pity about the owner. No matter, they would never meet again. For some reason goosebumps chased across her skin as she thought she heard a faintly mocking laugh echoing distantly, then she shrugged it off as part of her exhaustion.

🝆🝆🝆🝆🝆🝆

Jenny was idly wondering where Rachel was, when the bedroom door slowly opened, and her sister's pink face peered out.

"Hi! You're home early, aren't you? What happened?" She came out closing the door tightly behind her.

"Why are you acting so furtively?" Jenny asked, pushing herself up from her lounging position, and regarded Rachel with growing suspicion. Then it dawned on her, and she said accusingly, "You've got someone in there, haven't you?"

Her sister looked suitably guilty as she tried to justify herself. "Okay, you have caught me, but this is not simply a casual fling. We're serious about each other. I have been wanting you to meet him, and I guess now is as good a time as any to introduce you. James, come on out and meet my sister."

Rachel opened the bedroom door and pulled him forward. A tall, dark-haired handsome man, with a strangely familiar look, came out with a slightly embarrassed air and walked towards her, smiling sheepishly. "I'm very pleased to meet you at last. Rachel is always extolling your virtues, and I started to wonder if you were real, or perhaps just a figment of her imagination."

"What on earth has she been saying about me?" Jenny shook his hand and laughed.

"You'd be surprised," he grinned. "Are you saying that you don't really wear a halo?"

"I really don't, not that I'm aware of anyway," she smiled. Jenny turned to her sister, with a humorous frown. "Honestly, Rachel, you do exaggerate at times. My virtues are many, but sainthood is not one of them."

Rachel giggled at her sister's exasperated expression, and blushed, as she changed the subject by twining her arm through the boyfriends and edged him closer to Jenny. "Well, Jen, what do you think of my handsome hunk?"

Now it was his turn to look embarrassed. "I think I'll just leave and let you girls get on with whatever it is that girls get on with." He planted a quick kiss on Rachel's upturned lips and waved at Jenny, as he gathered a briefcase and jacket up. "See you, gorgeous. Two days and I'll be back. Bye, Jenny, nice to have met you. I wish it had been under better circumstances." Then he was gone, and now the flat seemed empty. James had seemed to fill the place.

"My goodness, Rachel, he is a big built guy."

"A bit overwhelming, isn't he?" Rachel smiled, happily.

ꗞ ꗞ ꗞ ꗞ ꗞ ꗞ

During the next two days, the girls regaled each other with stories of their respective activities. As Jenny came to the end of her traumatic experiences on holiday, Rachel, who was already laughing so much she was crying, doubled over at the image of Jenny fleeing in a taxi, wearing dark glasses and with a scarf draped over her head.

"I can't believe this is you we're talking about. Things like that just don't happen to you, and a naked man clutching you in front of everyone, which you must admit is quite unusual. You are normally so quiet and well-behaved and... Well, sort of mouse-like. I don't mean that in an unkind way," she tacked on hastily, dabbing at her brimming eyes with a tissue.

"I know you don't, sis," Jenny laughed. "And you're right, in a way. My life is not usually very exciting, I'm afraid."

"So, you found him exciting, did you?" her sister sniggered.

"I was too embarrassed to find that unfortunate episode exciting," Jenny scolded her.

"Don't you feel that you would like to break out sometimes, do something different with your life?" Rachel asked her, curiously.

"Different was what my holiday turned out to be," Jenny smiled. "That will last me a lifetime, thank you." They both collapsed with laughter again. When they had sobered up, Jenny looked thoughtfully at her sister. "Seriously, Rachel, how much does this relationship with James mean to you? How dependable is he?" This was not just an idle question; Jenny did not want to see Rachel rush into a relationship again without thinking carefully about it first. "How long have you known him and why haven't I heard about him before?"

"Honestly, Jen, I've mentioned him on numerous occasions, but you were always so immersed in your work and hardly ever listened to me, so I just gave up bothering. I decided that there would be time enough for you to get to know him when I started bringing him home, and now you have finally met him. Only not in the way I had anticipated." Her sister sat forward, with her hands cupping her face, and rubbing her cheeks. "Oh! God, Jen, I love James desperately and I am quite sure he feels the same. He is talking about taking me over to Staunton to meet with his family. Surely that must mean he thinks a great deal of me, doesn't it?"

Jenny gazed at her sister's lovely face and hoped for her sake that James really was serious about Rachel, and not just swayed by her looks. Rachel might end up being hurt. She had suffered setbacks before, and Jenny could not bear her to endure another.

"Tell me more about him," she demanded.

Rachel eagerly enthused about her wonderful man. His eldest brother owned a large share in the lucrative family business, also owned smaller companies, and advised others, which indicated that he was quite wealthy in his own right, as were the whole family. He was taking James under his wing, not because he particularly wanted to, but as a favour to his parents. He sounded overbearing and pompous and as his description went on, an alarm bell somewhere deep in Jenny's brain began to give a faint ring. Especially when Rachel informed her that his brother had been staying in the countryside and mentioned the very same county as she herself had stayed in. Coincidences like this did not happen, did they?

"Um, does James resemble his brother much?" Jenny asked, nonchalantly.

"Apparently he does," Rachel smiled. "He's got two other brothers as well, all tall and dark. I've not met them yet, but he tells me that they are all large men."

She looked puzzled when a blush spread over her sister's face. Jenny had left out some of the more embarrassing details while telling her story and now was glad she had done so. "Well!" Jenny announced, jumping up and changing the subject, "I think we could both do with some supper, it's getting late, and we've got work tomorrow."

As she made the coffee, Jenny speculated about James and his brothers. There were plenty of tall dark men about and a great deal of people chose Devon as a place to holiday in. It would be an incredibly small world if that man really turned out to be James's brother, so she would dismiss the whole episode from her mind, and file it away as an amusing holiday anecdote.

੫ ੫ ੫ ੫ ੫ ੫

Early the next morning, Jenny opened the door of the shop and listened with pleasure to the old-fashioned bell, she never got tired of hearing it, it reminded her of a bygone age, a far gentler era. Sometimes Jenny felt as though she had been born out of time, because this age was far too hectic for her. She usually looked forward to being in the shop, but the thought of bumping into Jason again filled her with apprehension.

Rachel and her usually took turns in opening the shop. One did the clearing up in the flat, while the other dealt with the first few customers, so Jenny sat on a stool, waiting for the first customer of the morning. She knew it would be old Mr Transcombe; he was as regular as clockwork. He would come in, look around at the same old books that they never got rid of, say the same words, and smile happily as he left, yet he never bought a thing. Jenny smiled, he was a lonely old man, and she did not begrudge him his moments of pleasure. Her smile widened as the bell went and there he was as usual.

The morning wore on and Jenny stretched tiredly. For some reason, it had been particularly busy, and she was looking forward to breaking for lunch. Today Rachel would not be down until the afternoon, it was her day for attacking the heavy cleaning and she always took twice as long as Jenny. She walked to the door to put the lock on and paused to admire the way sunlight glanced off a small glass vase, reflecting a myriad of sparkling colours onto the wall behind it. The design it formed gave her another idea for her artwork, and Jenny smiled as she worked on it in her head. She filed it away in the back of her mind, as Jenny remembered what she had been about to do. As she lifted her arm to push the bolt home on the top of the door, Jason pressed the handle down and pushed past her into the shop. Her heart sank and she sighed wearily.

"What do you want, Jason?" she asked, trying hard to be polite and friendly.

"Come and have lunch with me," he begged, gazing at her with pleading eyes.

Jenny nearly gave in as she heard the desperation in his voice, but she hardened her heart. "I'm sorry, Jason, I don't leave the shop for lunch," she said firmly. This was not strictly true, but he was not to know that. Jenny did not want to give him the slightest encouragement, and she knew that even lunching with Jason might give him the wrong idea, and she did not want to lead him on.

Jason was beginning to become persistent again and she was relieved when she was, quite literally, saved by the bell. The door pushed open once again and her sister rushed in waving a letter in her hand.

"Jenny, guess what?" Rachel was bubbling with excitement. "I've been offered a teaching post, and it's local. I can't believe it. Only temporary, but it will do until I get a permanent placing." She put her arms around Jenny and hugged her ecstatically, twirling her madly around.

"For goodness sake calm down, Rachel," Jenny laughed, pulling herself free, then turned and held the door open pointedly. "You will have to excuse us, Jason, we have much to discuss. Enjoy your lunch, won't you?" She gave him a tight smile as he reluctantly departed. Both girls stood frowning, as they watched him walk down the narrow path, and out to the pavement.

"Is he still being a pain, Jen?" Rachel asked.

"He won't take no for an answer. I can't seem to make him understand that I'm just not interested," Jenny rolled her eyes. "I can't see me taking *him* home to mother, can you?"

They laughed conspiratorially together as they began to reminisce about various appalling boyfriends they had tried to make their parents accept, and the resigned expression on their mother's face whenever they had brought someone home. Then discussed Rachels's good news. Jenny was relieved to know that Rachel would not be taking up the teaching post until the end of the summer holidays when the new term began, so she would still be able to help run the shop. Jenny wondered how she would cope managing it by herself when the time came, with the added headache of trying to create a collection of innovative designs. There were always the evenings, she supposed. She could fit her designing in between dinner and supper.

 finishing ♫ ♫ ♫ ♫ ♫ ♫

James was in his brother's study, and Darius reluctantly took his concentration away from the screen on the desk in front of him. "Yes, you were saying?"

"Oh, you actually heard me then?" James said sarcastically.

"I did! Something about your latest conquest, I believe. Right, go ahead."

"Your words make it sound sordid. It was not a conquest; it was a mutual attraction. Rachel and I were drawn towards each other, and everything fell into place. I love her. You ought to see her, Darius, she is beautiful. Rachel is everything you could ask for in a woman and she loves me," James enthused, his smile dying as he caught the sceptical look on his brother's face. "Honestly, Darius, you've got no romance in your soul. Don't you believe that someone could actually love me?"

"It's not them, it's you," his brother snorted. "What about the string of broken romances behind you, remember them? How many times have I had to bail you out of a tricky situation?"

James shrugged his shoulders, but he did have the grace to look slightly ashamed. "This is different. I really love her, and I mean deeply. I've never been this way before, and you know it." He looked pleadingly at his brother. "You have to meet her, Darius. She's a really nice girl."

His brother stared at him, taken aback by the vehemence in his voice. James really did seem to mean it, so was this the real thing at last? Darius just hoped this girl was not taking his brother for a ride, because James stood to inherit quite a great deal of money one day and his brother was, he thought, at the age of twenty-three, a bit too young and irresponsible for such a deep commitment. Darius decided that he would be all too happy to meet this paragon of virtue and judge for himself. "Very well, bring her over one evening for a meal, but give me due warning and I will make sure to be here."

"Great! I'll do just that," James grinned, satisfied that he had got his way.

Darius gave a slight grimace. To his eyes, his brother looked so young and impressionable. He could only hope this girl turned out to be as innocent as she had been described, and not a schemer, as he suspected.

"Anyway, enough about me." James's voice penetrated his thoughts. "What has been happening to you? I was going to ask if you had enjoyed your holiday, but by the state of your nose and hand, it didn't turn out too well. What the devil happened to you?"

"Where do I begin," Darius sighed. "Well, let's just say I am lucky that the local headlines don't read, 'Lustful, depraved pervert tries to rob innocent maiden of virtue,' or, 'Vengeful woman got her own back on man who molested her.'"

James regarded him with growing disbelief as Darius went on to describe all the punishment he had suffered at her hands.

"You? Old stick-in-the-mud Darius, never," his brother laughed. "I can't believe all that happened to you." James laughed even more heartily, as he regarded his brother's straight face.

"It wasn't that funny," said Darius huffily. "It was like a waking nightmare; I can only think that somewhere I've got an arch-enemy who has made a pact with the devil and had him unleash one of his minions upon me. Well, it worked. I have not shown my face at the office or anywhere else for four days. Apart from my swollen nose, my hand is virtually useless now having to wear this darned splint and look here." Darius stood up gingerly, untucked his shirt and pulled it up, showing James the multicoloured bruise that ran the length of his torso.

"Wow, now that is some painful looking bruise," his brother said, giving a surprised whistle. "How did it happen?"

"That's where the ground hit me when she made me fly off the hill."

"You make her sound like a witch." James could not help it, his laughter verged on the hysterical. "I'm sorry, Darius, I know it's probably darn painful, but are you sure all this was caused by one small woman?"

"Yep, all one woman." Darius looked back at him, and his own lips twitched. His mind conjured her up, small, pretty face, huge green eyes, tangle of long brown curly hair, good figure. Exceptionally good figure. He paused as his mind lingered, and a tide of red surged into his face as he remembered the last time he had seen her. He had stood mesmerised like an idiotic gawking schoolkid. Heaven knows what it must have looked like to Gina and that moronic manager, but if he had been going to commit some indecent act, didn't they think he would have kept his voice down? He rubbed his neck tiredly and winced, as he realised that he had used his injured hand, cursing her all over again.

Darius was a man who valued his privacy. He was quiet, controlled, severe at times, very rarely went to parties, and spent his leisure time immersed in new business projects. He had managed, up to the age of thirty-four, to avoid commitment and embarrassment, yet in four short days he had not only been called a pervert, but he had also hunched naked in front of a crowd of people and sustained injuries that even years of skiing and various sports had never inflicted upon him.

Darius shook his head, groaning at the haunting memory, and sank back down into his chair. "Remind me never to go on holiday again."

"Don't let this small setback put you off." James was still chuckling. He laughed as his brother raised his eyebrows. "Well, okay, traumatic time. Seriously, Darius, we had enough trouble persuading you to take even that small break. You needed a rest."

"I know," Darius smiled at his concerned face. "But I think I can rest just as well at home, thanks. At least I'm safe here."

Fate heard his confident words and laughed mockingly at him.

Chapter Five

Jenny was helping Rachel pack her small holdall. Her sister had been invited to meet the rest of James's family and was feeling extremely nervous about meeting them all.

"Why can't you come with me, Jen? I'm sure they won't mind."

"No, I can't leave my designs for a while." Jenny shook her head at her sister's pleading eyes. "I have got some very lucrative commissions, and the shop must be kept open. Anyway, I couldn't just turn up uninvited. They might not appreciate that. So go, have fun, and if they look down their noses at you, they will have me to answer to."

Although Jenny said it lightly and laughed, she was not too sure she liked the sound of the older brother. It seemed to her that he was too arrogant and demanding, but then maybe James being the younger was just a little jealous, so she should reserve judgement. If this affair developed into something more serious, she would be bound to meet him at some stage in the relationship, and they would at least have to be civil to one another.

꒰꒱꒰꒱꒰꒱

While Rachel was away, Jenny kept herself busy trying to fit her designing in with running the shop, and at night she tidied the flat. She had fallen into a routine and was coping far better than she had anticipated. This evening, she stood looking around at the faded wallpaper and frowned. "It could do with a good overhaul," Jenny muttered to herself.

If she started to decorate it tonight, she stood a good chance of finishing it before her sister got back, and it would be a pleasant surprise for Rachel. Having decided, Jenny put thought into action, and rolling her sleeves up, set to with determination and had soon stripped three of the walls. A quick glance at the time reminded her of how late it was becoming, and Jenny decided that it was time to call a halt.

As Jenny climbed down off the ladder, the phone rang. Who would call her at this late hour? Panic set in. Could it be her parents? Had something awful happened, or was Rachel in trouble? She rushed over to the coffee table where she had left the phone under a sheet to keep it free of dust, and scrabbled to find it.

"Yes!" Jenny snapped, as she snatched the phone up. There was the sound of heavy breathing and she felt a frisson of alarm. The breathing increased and she could hear what sounded like a grunt, then a snuffling sound followed. Jenny had heard all the rumours about these people, cranks who indulged their fantasies like this. She spoke at the same time as the masculine voice on the other end, drowning him out. "You pervert! People like you make me sick. Get off my phone before I call the police."

Her heart jumped, as a man's voice replied coldly, "Obviously, I have the wrong number. I was trying to contact a Jenny Stayner, and I am not a pervert, madam, I have an extremely heavy cold!" Then with a resounding thud, the phone went dead. Jenny put it down slowly, staring at it in utter embarrassment.

On the receiving end, Darius sat with an odd expression on his face. This was the second time in just one month that a woman had called him a pervert. If he didn't know better... No. Darius shook his head. It surely could not be her or was she haunting him? Unless he really was cracking up, and he needed another break after all.

Jenny put her hands over her face. Oh, lord, if that was James's brother, what must he think of her? She dropped her hands and brightened. It was okay, he had thought it was a wrong number. Thank heavens for that, Jenny thought in relief. Yet the deep tone of his voice had set her nerve ends tingling. It had an oddly familiar sound. Could it...? No, impossible.

ꔄ ꔄ ꔄ ꔄ ꔄ ꔄ

The next day Jenny closed early and got to grips with the decorating, she was in the middle of stripping the last wall, when the ring of the doorbell startled her. Again, it was late, and Jenny tutted with vexation as she scrambled down the ladder. She opened the door cautiously keeping the chain on, and was shocked to see, as she peered through the gap, the same elegant woman who had accompanied the unfortunate man at the hotel. Her mouth opened and an embarrassed, "Oh," escaped on a dismal sigh.

The woman looked as taken aback as she did, and Jenny pulled herself together. "I'm sorry, I was just so surprised to see you. Can I help you?" Her internal alarm bell gave another jangle. Coincidence was alive and well and standing right in front of her, and an ominous sign that her suspicions were about to be confirmed by her unexpected visitor.

"My God!" The other woman gave her a faint smile. "This is some coincidence. You are Jenny, I take it?"

Jenny eyed her warily, feeling at a disadvantage. This woman had addressed her by name. "Should I know you?"

"You mean apart from the disastrous meeting we last had?" The woman smiled more fully, as Jenny blushed. The woman asked if she could come in and have a word with her, and she laughed as Jenny hesitated, before taking the chain off the door. "It's quite all right, I assure you that I'm not violent. I'm not going to beat you up for punishing my brother. Accidents happen, right?"

"That many in so short a time?" Jenny said, with a faint grimace.

"Yes, weird, isn't it, and how coincidental is this? Things appear to have come full circle." The other woman stared at her thoughtfully, suppressing a smile.

"Full circle?" Jenny said, puzzled.

"As in extremely odd to be meeting again. It might help to clarify the situation if I explain why I'm here. I'm Gina, James's sister, and I said that I would call in and meet you while I was over this way, so you see that is where the vagaries of life come into play. We have already met. Strange huh?"

"It really is!" Jenny let her in, lost for words, hardly able to believe that the coincidence she had laughed off, was in fact a reality, and remembering with embarrassment exactly how much of her Gina had seen when they last met.

"I am to extend an invitation to you. Next time Rachel visits, please feel free to accompany her," Gina said, making herself comfortable in one of the small armchairs. She hesitated. "Mind you, having realised who you are, it might be best if it's when Darius is away."

"Darius?" Jenny remembered his name, but made an effort to look blankly at the other woman, and Gina's smile widened.

"He's our older brother, I believe you've met him, in the flesh, so to speak." Her laughter pealed out at the horror-struck look on the young woman's face.

"Oh, my God, this is just too awful," Jenny moaned, all her worst fears confirmed. Suspecting it was vastly different from being told to her face by his sister that it was true, and she looked across at the other woman with a glum expression. The alarm bell was having a field day. She sank down onto the sofa and then sat forward anxiously, saying glumly. "I simply cannot face him again. It might be better if I never visit, because there is always the chance that we may meet if I do. I don't know why this is happening to me. My life was fairly quiet and uneventful until now." She thought of Jason. "Well, reasonably so, until recently."

She caught Gina's inquiring look and found herself explaining about Jason's unwelcome attention. "What you want is another man!" Gina told her.

"Another man?" Jenny repeated, staring at her as though she were quite mad. "My life is quite complicated enough as it is, thank you."

"I haven't taken leave of my senses," Gina laughed. "What I meant was you need to let this Jason think that you are keeping company with another man. Perhaps he will take the hint then."

"This is so weird," Jenny smiled. "I've only just met you, yet here I am telling you my life history. You must be totally bored."

"No, I'm not bored at all. I like you. Be flattered, I don't like many people," Gina smiled back at her. She stood up and studied the girl on the sofa, comparing Jenny to the photograph on the wall of a blonde girl standing beside her in the picture. "Your sister is quite beautiful."

"Yes, Rachel takes after my mother," Jenny smiled.

"You aren't much alike, are you?" she stated, studying the tall, elegant Rachel. She turned back and caught a slightly pained expression on Jenny's face. "I don't mean you aren't attractive, you know. I wasn't making an unfavourable comparison."

"It's okay," Jenny smiled. "I know that Rachel is quite lovely and I'm proud of that. My sister is not a vain person and besides, she is so nice that I couldn't be jealous even if I wanted to."

Gina stared at her in surprise. Jenny really had no idea of how pretty she was, so not a vain girl then. She gave a small nod to herself, wondering if Darius had finally met his match. Jenny might not think she was attractive, but her brother had been totally preoccupied with this girl ever since that disastrous holiday. It was the first time he had taken this much notice of a female, apart from his cold-blooded dalliances that occurred from time to time. She thought of Melissa and her lips tightened. The fact that he spent an awful lot of time saying what he would like to do to this girl if he ever got his hands on her was beside the point. Anyway, boiling in oil was illegal. It was the most animated she had seen him in a long time, and it was good to see. Gina glanced down at her watch as she broke out of her reverie.

"Oh, heavens, I have an appointment to keep. Now, I simply must fly. I will just make it if I rush. Now don't forget, accept the invitation, and come and see us. You will meet the rest of the mob then." Gina saw the doubtful look on Jenny's face and assured her that she would make sure the coast was clear. Then she was gone in a flurry of silk and perfume.

ɯ ɯ ɯ ɯ ɯ ɯ

Jenny slumped down again feeling worn out. Gina was like a whirlwind, she was so full of life and her presence had overwhelmed Jenny, now she needed time to mull over the conversation. Life was so strange, she thought. Gina had been a stranger such a short while ago, now it seemed that she could become much more if James and Rachel became a permanent fixture.

Jenny swept the pile of wallpaper up, leaving the room in a reasonably fit state to sit in. After washing the sticky grime off her hands, she produced a quick meal and devoured it hungrily, then sat nursing a small white wine while giving some thought to the mythical man she was supposed to produce. It was a great idea in theory. The fact was how did Jenny set about acquiring one? She could hardly rush up to the first presentable male and ask. "Excuse me, you handsome devil, you'll do. Will you come out with me?"

Jenny laughed. She could see that leading to all sorts of trouble. Her colour came up, as a powerful, naked body superimposed itself on her mind. "For God's sake, get a grip of yourself, girl. You won't ever see him again and anyway, he's just a man," she muttered. Yes, but he is also the brother of your sister's boyfriend, her brain reminded her. No escaping that unpalatable fact. Her mind was getting overactive as his image appeared again, so Jenny told her brain to change the subject and jumped to her feet, setting to vigorously with the rest of the wall. She might as well finish it, because there was no way she would be able to sleep just yet, not after Gina's unsettling visit.

ɯ ɯ ɯ ɯ ɯ ɯ

When Rachel came back, she was so rapturous about having met with James's family that she did not even notice the new wallpaper. Jenny looked at her with a trace of disappointment. So much for all my hard work, she thought wryly. She sat Rachel down, made her a welcome cup of coffee and seating herself comfortably opposite her sister, demanded to hear all about her visit. Jenny decided that it might be a sensible idea to keep Gina's visit to herself. It would only upset Rachel if she learned of her sister's first unfortunate meeting with Darius.

"The parents were away, but the others were so nice to me Jen, so welcoming. His brothers are all terribly good looking, all except the oldest one. Well, I suppose he is very handsome really, but he is so aloof, and he doesn't smile much. His sister didn't have much to say either. I got the impression that she found me a bit too young and silly, and you know how it is. If you think someone sees you in that light, you invariably end up acting exactly the way they would expect, but she was kind." She sighed and then smiled. "Anyway, it was great. James seemed to be proud of me."

"What about Darius, his elder brother," Jenny asked casually. "What did he think of you?"

"Well, it's hard to know what he thought, because he didn't talk much at all." Her sister's smile died. "He was terribly polite, of course, but I felt as though he was quietly judging me. I found him a bit overpowering really."

Jenny felt a surge of protective anger course through her. What was not to like about Rachel? Her sister was exactly as she appeared to be, open, honest, and natural.

"I didn't say he didn't like me, Jen, or made me feel unwelcome, so don't go all overprotective on me," her sister said, as she saw the set look on her face. She put her arm through Jenny's, and gazed around the room, only then becoming aware of the change. "Oh, Jen, it's so pretty.

Terrific job, sis. You must have worked like crazy to get this finished in time."

"I sure did and I'm glad that you're suitably impressed." Jenny smiled, as Rachel stared at the wallpaper appreciatively. Her smile withered rapidly, as her sister added blithely. "At least James's brother and sister won't see the old, faded paper when they arrive."

"Let me get this straight, you have invited his brother and sister down to see us?" Jenny said, aghast. She calmed herself, as she remembered that James had more than one brother.

"Which brother would this be?"

"Darius, you know, the older one," Rachel informed her airily, not noticing the horror-struck look that appeared on her sister's face and then flopped onto the sofa pulling Jenny down beside her, and waved her arm round at the room. "Don't worry, sis, it looks really presentable now you've freshened it up. Besides, it's us they're visiting. I don't suppose they care about the state of the flat."

Jenny sat down slowly, suddenly feeling old, and looked helplessly at her. What could she say? "I have seen more of James's brother, much more than I want to." She flushed at the persistent image. What had happened to the promise that Gina had made to make sure their paths would never cross? Then Jenny thought about Rachel's airy way of arranging things and knew without being told that, somehow, she must have conveyed the impression to Gina that Jenny would love to meet her brother, and to be fair, Rachel had no inkling about why it was not such a good idea. Somehow, she would have to contrive to be absent when he arrived.

For one mad moment she even thought of making a date with Jason, but dismissed the idea as quickly as it had entered her mind. Jenny had enough problems without adding to them.

֍֍֍֍֍֍

When the threatened visit drew near, Jenny mustered up her courage, saying to her sister with regret, "Look, I'm sorry, Rachel, but something has come up, and I have to take some of my designs up to town. Special order, so it's worth a lot of money to me, and I can't really miss this opportunity."

"Do you mean to say that you are leaving me to cope alone with them?" Her sister frowned at her. "What can I say about your absence? It looks so rude, Jen, after me arranging it, and you know how much this means to me. If you are worried about meeting them, don't be, they are really nice people."

"I just can't, Rachel." Jenny shook her head dumbly. For the first time since they were small girls, she saw real anger on her sister's face.

"Surely you can do this for me. It's not much to ask, is it? You needn't stay the whole time. You can use the shop as an excuse to pop out for a while to take a break. After all, you're using your work as an excuse now, aren't you!" Rachel stood with her hands on her hips looking hurt and upset, which of course produced a twinge of guilt in Jenny, so she gave in.

"Oh, very well. I can phone and arrange another meeting, I suppose, and try and explain it away. I just hope nothing goes wrong," she said in despair.

"Thanks, Jen, and why would things not go well?" Her sister said, hugging her. She moved back and looked at Jenny with a kind smile. "You mustn't try and avoid them, you know. They're not ogres and I'm sure they'll like you. Don't underestimate yourself like this." Rachel, as usual, had got it all wrong. She always assumed that Jenny's quietness masked a deep shyness. What she could not understand was that although Jenny liked people, she was happy with her own company. She didn't particularly like gatherings or formal dos as Rachel did, and was quite content to potter about in her workroom on her own.

Another thing she could hardly point out was that in this instance, the one man she most wanted to avoid was the very one they had laughed so hysterically over. Her sister would certainly not be smiling now if she knew. Jenny sighed, no getting out of this. The ordeal would have to be faced she supposed.

When the great day came, Jenny felt as though royalty were about to descend. Rachel was fluttering about, looking harassed, fiddling with the table settings, and bemoaning the tiny size of the dining room.

"For heaven's sake, Rachel, calm down. Who was it that said they are only coming to see us, not the flat? Now sit down and have a sip of wine." She pushed her sister onto the sofa and poured her a small drink, then picked a jacket up and headed for the door, ignoring Rachel's curious frown. "I won't be long."

"Jenny?" her sister said, suspicion forming on her face.

"I've just got to go down to the workroom to check on some designs," Jenny called, as she shut the door quickly behind her. Their guests were about due and if she timed it right, they would be gone when she returned. Rachel would have to serve the meal without her and would never forgive her, of course, but at this moment it was the best possible course to take. The thought of meeting that man again filled Jenny with a sense of horror, and something else that she would rather not analyse.

Jenny was deeply absorbed, sorting through some new paints she had ordered. She spread them out on the counter in the shop and stood with her back to the door, which Jenny realised she had forgotten to lock when the bell tinkled.

"Hello," a deep masculine voice said.

Jenny stiffened. She had heard that voice before, a bit higher pitched in pain, of course, but the same voice. She felt goosebumps rise on her scalp and slowly turned. They stared at each other in appalled fascination. He was the first to break the tense growing silence.

"You!" Darius exclaimed, with something akin to horror. "Oh, no, please tell me that you are just a customer here, and not who I think you are?"

Jenny finally found her voice. "Who else would I be at this time of the evening, and why are you here in the shop? I have deliberately kept out of your way, so anything that happens to you now is strictly not my fault." She folded her arms and glared at him.

He glared back, shaking his head in disbelief. "Out of the goodness of my heart, I decided to come and seek out this, 'shy little thing,' who was so scared of meeting us," he snorted. "If I had known it was my nemesis, I would have run the other way."

"Pity you didn't and kept going!" she shot back.

Jenny clutched her arms to stop herself from shaking. My goodness, Darius was a big man. When he was standing upright, that is, she thought, gazing up at him. Jenny pressed a hand to her head as a provoking memory resurfaced. For pity's sake, will you stop resurrecting that image she pleaded with her mind as a blush spread over her face. When Jenny glanced up at Darius, she was surprised to see a matching flush suffusing his, and it made her feel even worse.

"Please go," she stammered. His presence was overwhelming Jenny, and she desperately wanted him out of her shop. She heard the soft click of heels approaching the door from the side path, guessing that it would be Rachel coming to check on her, and Jenny did not want her sister to know that she and Darius had met before.

"Go away," she hissed. "My sister knows nothing of our previous encounter."

"Don't worry," he snapped. "Nothing will give me greater pleasure."

Darius snatched the door open and went to march out, turned to say something else, thought better of it and began to turn again. Jenny could only watch in growing horror, as his heel caught the edge of the old, frayed doormat, and almost in slow motion, he toppled backwards out of the door. She snapped out of her mesmerised trance as his head hit the gravel path with a resounding thud, and he lay still. Jenny ran over to him and knelt, then gently ran her hands over his shoulders and head. Her fingers encountered the unmistakable sticky feel of blood and she gulped with fear.

"That's it! What I started on holiday, I've finally finished. I've killed him."

Rachel came from around the side of the shop and skidded to a halt, her hand on her mouth with shock at the scene confronting her.

"What on earth happened? Is he conscious, shall I call an ambulance?"

As she spoke, Darius stirred and groaned. "No ambulance." Then his hands automatically moved towards the source of the pain. A sharp smack on his arm prevented the movement.

"Leave your head alone and keep still," Jenny commanded. "You could have fractured your skull."

His eyes shot open at the sound of her voice. "What is it with you? Do you have some sort of fetish and like the sight of my blood on your hands? Have you got a small waxen image of me, by any chance, that you stick pins in?"

She stared at him in concern. He was obviously rambling. The injury must be more serious than she had thought. "Please don't talk, just relax." Jenny put her hand out to stroke his forehead, causing him to shrink back, with an apprehensive expression.

"Don't you dare lay a finger on me. Who knows what further damage you may inflict."

Her concern deepened. He really was in shock. She would have to call his sister and then she realised with alarm that he was levering himself up into a sitting position. "No, you must stay still. You could have a serious injury." Jenny leant towards him.

"Not yet, I haven't, but if I stay here any longer, I will have," he grunted, backing away warily.

Rachel was following this exchange with a bemused expression. Why was he talking to her sister like this? Anyone would think that Jenny had deliberately caused his accident.

"Now look here, Darius, I don't care if you are James's brother, I won't have you talk to her like this! After all, it wasn't my sister's fault that you tripped and fell. You do seem to be accident prone, don't you?" She looked meaningfully at his bandaged hand and bruised nose.

Darius gazed at her with disbelief, grunted with exasperation, then sighed. Rachel was not to know about his previous encounters with her sister. He levered himself to his feet and stood up swaying slightly, as Gina came hastily along the path.

"Oh! Darling, what's happened now?" She grasped his arm with concern and looked from him to Jenny. "Uh, oh! Met again, I see?"

"You didn't tell me you knew him, Jen." Rachel looked shocked and mystified.

"Remember my disastrous holiday?" Jenny's shoulders sagged guiltily, and she looked steadily at her sister. Rachel stared at her uncomprehendingly. Then her face filled with horror as enlightenment dawned. "Oh, no, this is the man who...?" Her voice became strangled. "Why did it have to be him, James's brother? Oh... Jenny."

To everyone's consternation, Rachel burst into tears and ran inside, slamming the door and leaving them all staring after her.

Gina broke the strained silence. "Well," she said brightly. "Perhaps the next visit will turn out better."

Two faces turned to her with utter disbelief, and her smile faded as she became businesslike again. "Right, we had better get you home, Darius, and see to that head wound. It doesn't look too bad to me, but we should get the doctor to check it over." Then, in an aside to Jenny, she tacked on, "I'll sort it out. Tell Rachel not to worry, she won't be condemned to purgatory by the family, and I will try and persuade him that you are not really a witch." Gina smiled conspiratorially at Jenny, and laughing merrily, led a disgruntled Darius away.

Jenny stood watching them until they were out of sight. This was all her fault. The accident had happened because she had tried to avoid him, and Jenny felt nervous and guilty as she went to confront her sister. An explanation was in order.

Rachel was huddled forlornly in one of the small armchairs, a handkerchief pressed to her face, and she raised red and swollen eyes as Jenny entered.

"Oh, Jen, why did it have to be him of all people? What will James think of me? He'll think I've got a severely disturbed sister. One who hates men," Rachel gulped, as she saw her sister's woebegone face. Her lips trembled and a faint smile surfaced, as the humour of the situation hit her. "Sorry, Jen, none of this is your fault."

"It is, in a way, and I feel terrible. Every time I get near the poor man, something dreadful happens." Jenny paused and sat down, uttering a heavy sigh of regret, and gave her sister a weak smile. "It doesn't matter now. He and I will probably never meet again. Anyway, it's you and James who are important. Darius can't condemn you just because he thinks I've put a hex on him."

Rachel sniggered. "That poor man, he must think that you're out to get him. You're probably right, it's better that you don't meet too often."

Jenny laughed as she visualised Darius holding a cross out if he caught sight of her again. "Seriously, Rachel, forget this, forget me, and enjoy your relationship with James. His brother is my problem."

Chapter Six

The shop was doing well, thought Jenny, as she cashed up the money from the till. Most people paid by card now, but there were the few who still preferred to pay by cash, and she must get to the bank before it closed. She glanced up at Rachel to inform her that she was just leaving. Her sister was rearranging the shelves looking absorbed and happy. Obviously, her relationship with James was flourishing if her glowing face was anything to judge by.

A few weeks had passed since Jenny's last unfortunate encounter with Darius. She had found out through Rachel that he had some stitches put in the wound to his head, which made her feel incredibly guilty. She knew good manners dictated that she really ought to send him a small note of apology, but Jenny could not bring herself to make contact with him, so she left it, and as time went by, she was able to push him to the back of her mind.

The invitation when it came shocked Jenny out of her hard-won composure and even made her contemplate booking another holiday.

"We are both invited to attend Dominic's birthday party." Rachel held it up, waving it happily. She saw Jenny's puzzled look. "You know, the next brother up from James."

"Will Darius be there?"

"I should think so. After all, he does live there," her sister pointed out.

"Then I can't go!" Jenny said firmly.

"You have to, Jen, otherwise it will look as though you're snubbing them."

"Oh, no, not me. I'm not going anywhere near that man. I'm not setting foot in a house where he has even breathed," Jenny stated determinedly, putting her hands up in protest.

"Well, I shall phone and accept the invite for both of us." Rachel laughed. She grabbed her mobile up and fought Jenny off as she cried. "Don't you dare say that I'm going."

The conversation did not last long, and Rachel turned with a triumphant look on her face as she put the phone down. "We are going, both of us. Now don't go all huffy on me, Jen," she said, at the cross expression on her sister's face. "You will be quite safe, or should I say he will. Apparently, Darius has gone abroad on business and will miss the whole thing."

"Well, thank God for that," Jenny's shoulders sagged with relief. "The only problem is what on earth do his family think of me? They must have heard some lurid tales by now, you know, 'Does she practise the dark arts,' things like that."

"You say the weirdest things sometimes. You and Darius have just got off to a bad start, that's all." Rachel grinned, as Jenny rolled her eyes at this understatement.

ꔷꔷꔷꔷꔷꔷ

Jenny felt apprehensive as the party approached. The main problem was what to take. In the end, she bundled one decent dress, with shoes to match and a change of underwear in case of emergencies, into a small holdall. One had to be prepared for the unexpected. Darius might just throw a bucket of water over her if he came home early and saw her strutting about in his comfort zone. That arrogant beast looked as though he had zero tolerance for annoying females and would dispose of any that dared to disagree with him. She wondered if he ate his previous girlfriends or simply buried them. Jenny gave a faint snicker. Okay, maybe that observation was a bit over the top, although it would never surprise her if he did deal cold-bloodedly when the time came to discard them. She added some outdoor clothes to her bag. It was bound to be cold when they left later. Good enough, she thought.

Jenny glanced at the case her sister was packing, with disbelief. "Good grief, Rachel, how long are you planning on staying? You surely don't need all that for one party?"

Her sister busied herself folding the clothes neatly into the case and did not look up. "You never know. James did say that he might show me over the grounds if we got there early enough. I can hardly wear this, can I?" Rachel held her delicate party dress up and laughed.

ॶ ॶ ॶ ॶ ॶ ॶ

They duly arrived at James's house in the neighbouring village of Staunton and what a beautiful house it turned out to be. The building stood in its own grounds, surrounded by mature trees and shrubs. A long gravel drive swung in a perfect curve from one gate to another, with plenty of parking for any number of vehicles. The house itself sat glowing softly in the waning sunlight, and a low terrace ran along the front with four curved steps leading up to the impressively heavy wooden door.

The taxi which had deposited them drove away, and they stood gazing up in awe at the creeper-clad front of the large house. Jenny suddenly felt nervous and wished she had not weakened. Why had she let Rachel talk her into accepting?

Her sister tucked an arm through hers, as though to stop her from making a bolt for it. "Come on, Jen, they don't bite, and the one most likely to isn't here." Rachel laughed, as she propelled Jenny up to the door. It opened as they approached and they were met by Gina, who welcomed them in, then escorted them straight upstairs and showed them into a pretty guest room.

"Now please, make yourselves at home, girls. Through that door, you have your own little en-suite, and you will find the beds quite comfy if you feel the need to retire early. Sometimes these parties can get quite tiring." She smiled, waggled her fingers, and told them to come down when they were ready.

Jenny turned and glared suspiciously at her sister. "Why didn't you tell me we were expected to stay the night?"

"I thought you knew, and it's for the whole weekend." Rachel shrugged innocently, as she turned and studied her face in the mirror. She darted a guilty look at Jenny, whose image advanced menacingly towards her in the mirror.

"What? No wonder you packed so much, and you know I only came for the party. Honestly, Rachel!" She was furious and went over and sat down with a thump on the bed, looking distinctly disgruntled.

"Jen, I'm sorry, but I knew that you would find an excuse not to come had I told you. Please don't be cross."

Jenny stared at her sister in exasperation. She sighed and softened at Rachel's anxious expression. "Oh, well, I can always go for long walks I suppose to pass the time. The grounds are lovely here, aren't they?" She got up and crossed to the window, looking out at the wide expanse of lawn. Her gaze sharpened as Jenny thought she spotted a familiar figure near a group of trees, then relaxed as James strolled into view. "Look, Rachel, isn't that James?"

Her sister jumped to her feet with a happy smile on her face and looked down on her boyfriend. "I wondered where he had got to. He was supposed to meet me at the door. You know, to bolster my confidence before meeting the family again. They can be quite overwhelming when together. I guess we must have arrived sooner than he thought."

As they watched him walk up onto the terrace, a lovely red-haired vision in black lace, sauntered up to James and pressed against him, twining her arms lovingly around his neck. She gave him a passionate kiss, and he didn't exactly seem to be fighting her off.

Jenny glanced quickly at her sister, noting the stricken expression on her face. "Now, Rachel, don't go jumping to conclusions, give him a chance to explain. She could just be a cousin or family friend, or something." Her voice trailed off, and Jenny had to admit that his response had looked pretty damning, but appearances can be deceptive, she told herself. I mean, look at me, tussling with a naked man in front of an audience. They could be forgiven for thinking that she was enjoying the experience. Proof if needed that not all things were so easy to explain away, but hopefully James had a perfectly reasonable excuse to offer.

ಡ ಡ ಡ ಡ ಡ ಡ

The party was underway, and it was a lively affair. There were a lot of glamorous people milling about, and Jenny felt positively dowdy. She had never bothered much with dressing up but had always loved this neat little black dress. Now it looked cheap next to the obviously expensive gowns most of the other women were wearing. What Jenny did not realise is that many of those other women were regarding her with unconcealed envy, wondering who she was. She could not see herself as they did. Her mane of curly hair drew the men's eyes like a magnet, and her slim and lovely figure kept them there. Jenny looked elegant and natural. Her make-up had been kept to the bare minimum, her skin glowed and her large green eyes sparkled in the soft lighting. Jenny's only extravagance had been a pair of impossibly high, black strappy sandals, which set her slim legs off to perfection.

Rachel looked equally as lovely, her blonde hair was piled up into a casual topknot with wispy curls escaping and framing her face. She wore a slender sheath of sky-blue silk, and her jewellery was discreet yet expensive, it was the one thing Rachel had of any value and had been left to her by their grandmother. Jenny also sported a small chain with a diamond cross, her share in the same inheritance.

Jenny stayed glued to her sister's side, as James had not yet made an appearance, and she wanted to be there to support Rachel when he did finally show. She thought it extremely rude of him not to have made a point of being there for Rachel when they first arrived. What's more, he had quite some explaining to do about that kiss. An older well-groomed, and still attractive woman appeared and stood in front of them. "How do you do, I'm Ellen Langston." She smiled sweetly up at them, as she took their hands.

They regarded her silently, taken aback. Was this tiny woman really the mother of such tall, strapping sons?

"I'm their grandmother," she said, almost as though the woman could read their minds. She broke off and waved at one of her grandsons, who blew her a smiling kiss. "I had a lot to do with their upbringing, and they were quite a trial, let me tell you, but after all these years, we have a great understanding of each other, and I am very proud of each one of them."

The girls smiled at each other. It was more obvious now from her age, which could be seen more clearly in close-up, that she was the grandmother. Yet a forgivable error to think of her as the mother, because she was so slim, still very attractive, as was her manner, and her skin had the bloom of a much younger woman. They looked down into her twinkling blue eyes and smiled back.

"Sit down with me, my dears, my feet aren't so reliable as they were. They ache so easily these days." She beckoned them across to a couch. "Now, tell me all about yourselves." Ellen patted the seat beside her, then sat and watched their pretty young faces as they talked. They came across as very nice girls and she wondered if they would be able to handle Isabel, her daughter-in-law. Her lips tightened as Ellen thought of her, and then she dismissed the woman from her mind. This was a party, and she would enjoy it. Time enough for unpleasant thoughts later.

ꕤ ꕤ ꕤ ꕤ ꕤ ꕤ

Jenny sat listening to the hubbub of laughter and conversation around her and felt bored. Ellen had been commandeered by an elderly gentleman and whisked off to dance, and to her amazement, they were still going strong. Rachel was occupied with James and looked as though she would be that way for some time, so she guessed they must have made up their differences. It would be interesting to know how James had explained away his behaviour.

Jenny rose and slipped quietly away to explore the rest of the house. All the rooms were large and spacious and decorated in extremely good taste. She fell in love with the light and airy conservatory as she wandered among the different foliaged plants, admiring the exotic blooms on some of them. Yet Jenny felt overawed by the sheer size of the place and turned to the stairs, intending to seek the sanctuary of her room. As she placed one foot on the first step, her gaze was caught by the half-open door of a panelled room, and through the gap in the door she could see shelf upon shelf of books. Her interest was immediately aroused. There must be something of interest to read among so many volumes.

She entered the study and looked over at the large, padded chair, which crouched behind the desk. Was this where her unfortunate victim sat and conducted his numerous business transactions? She idly ran her hands over the desk and saw his face staring at her from a silver frame. How vain, to have your own photograph on your desk, Jenny thought disdainfully.

She studied his face and felt a strange tremor run through her, God, he was handsome. He was olive-skinned, with thick wavy black hair and eyes to match, his lips were almost beautiful. They were wide, the top one well defined, bottom one full, yet firm. It was a sensuous mouth. His jaw was chiselled and aggressive and his nose aquiline, an arrogant nose if ever she saw one, she thought. In fact, he was so good looking, he was unreal. Jenny frowned, she didn't trust men who were so attractive, they usually loved themselves so much that it left little room for anyone else. For some reason that made her feel sad, and she hurriedly put the picture down. It was of no interest to her; he could love himself to death for all she cared. 'Liar,' a tiny voice cried inside.

Jenny felt tired, so she sat down in an old armchair in the shadows cast by the one table lamp in the room. She leaned her head back and relaxed. The room was so quiet and peaceful, the solid old door effectively shutting the world out.

Jenny was sliding into a doze when a sound at the door disturbed her and made her sit up warily. As the door swung wide, she held her breath and froze as she saw Darius walk slowly in, yawning tiredly as he unbuttoned his jacket. He reached the desk, looked around the room and saw her. Stared hard for a moment, then shook his head and sat down, drawing a sheaf of papers from the briefcase he carried with him.

Jenny cleared her throat and his reaction shocked her. Darius jumped to his feet as though he had been shot, knocking his chair over in the process. It caught the back of his legs, and he sank to his knees, looking across at her over the top of his desk. "Oh, good lord, you're real. I thought you were just an awful figment of my imagination." He tried to stand and sank back again. "And by the way, I think you've broken my leg this time."

Jenny removed her hands from her mouth and rushed to help him up.

"Stand back," he yelled. "Don't even think about it. Hands off!"

Ellen and James, who had been escorting his grandmother up to her bedroom, had now appeared on the scene alerted by the crash of the chair. All they could see was the top of Darius's head, his dark hair falling over his eyes, one arm on top of the desk trying to lever himself up, the other held up as though warding Jenny off. James smothered a laugh, and his grandmother tut-tutted. "Darius, what on earth are you doing down there behind your father's desk? Get up this instant, you are worse than a child."

"Please, Gran, leave me to die alone," Darius sighed heavily. "And take that woman with you." He pointed an accusing finger at Jenny, who looked back at him with concern, and stepped nearer.

"Are you sure that you're all right?"

"Uh-uh! Not another step." He held his hand up again.

"Darius! What on earth are you gabbling about?" his grandmother demanded impatiently.

Darius felt like the small child his grandmother was accusing him of being, resting his head on the desk, as she chastised him. "Never mind, Gran, you wouldn't understand what this witch has done to me."

"There you go again, Darius, now stop this at once. Come, my dear, you will have to forgive my grandson. He seems to be in a befuddled state of mind."

His grandmother gave him one last admonishing glance and steered Jenny from the room, followed by a chuckling James, who now knew what the connection was between the two. Darius gazed at the door long after they had left. He felt stunned. How could one woman create so much havoc in his life? He rubbed his bruised shin vigorously to ease the pain. There would be another bruise forming there soon to join all the others. Despite himself, a smile began to form on his face, then he laughed aloud. The sound startled Darius. How long had it been since he had heard himself do that, he wondered.

ﬠ ﬠ ﬠ ﬠ ﬠ ﬠ

When morning came, Jenny cautiously descended the stairs. She could hear laughter coming from the dining room and listened out for a familiar deep velvet voice, but it was absent from the conversation, so she felt it safe to go in. The company looked up as she entered and greeted her with smiling friendliness. Jenny was embarrassed to see that they had nearly finished their breakfast and murmured her apologies.

"You were sleeping so peacefully, Jen, that I didn't like to disturb you," Rachel said apologetically. She saw the way Jenny glanced furtively around the room and gave a knowing laugh. "The coast is clear, sis; he got up early and left the house."

Jenny sagged with relief and joined the others at the table. She sat and let the conversation wash over her, enjoying the warm flow of good-natured banter between the brothers and Gina. She wondered if breakfast was just as relaxed with the dour Darius seated at the table. Jenny could imagine him glaring at them all if their laughter got out of hand, then sighed impatiently. There were much more interesting subjects to think about, she told herself. After their leisurely breakfast, Rachel and James wandered off, leaving Jenny to her own devices. She walked out of the back door and stood on the patio, gazing out at the expanse of fields and woodland that surrounded the house and sighed blissfully. There must be some lovely walks to be had out there.

She ran back upstairs and slipped a light jacket on, then she was quickly out again and set off to explore the grounds and those beckoning pathways. Following a narrow trail through the woods, she came to a small stream that meandered through the trees and decided to trace its course. Jenny entered a clearing, where she could more easily gain access to the water, walked across to the bank, and stood near the edge peering down. She was disappointed to see that here it had shrunk to little more than a ditch, the main stream having veered off into the more impenetrable woodland. As Jenny leaned forward to peer down, she lost her footing, teetering precariously on the edge of the small incline, then fell, seeing to her horror where she was about to land up, and there was no way she could save herself. She hit the soggy ground in an undignified heap, face down in the oozing mud.

"Damn and blast!" Jenny raged, as she tried to extricate herself from the clinging, vile-smelling muck and brambles.

A mocking masculine voice tutted from above her, and Jenny's head shot up nearly causing her to fall forward again. Darius laughed triumphantly down at her. "Well, well, grovelling at my feet, just where I want you. I won't try and rescue you, not in that state." He stepped forward and crowed. "How does it feel to be on the receiving end for once?"

His victory was short-lived, and Darius just had time to groan. "Oh, no," as his feet skidded on the slippery surface and he slid down heavily, falling with a satisfyingly squelching thud beside her.

Jenny laughed hysterically as he raised his dripping head. "Oh, thank goodness! Swamp man to the rescue," she tittered at the strange apparition facing her.

His head had sunk into the soft ooze and was caked with lumps of mud and clumps of rotten vegetation. Two white eyes opened in the surface, as he frantically tried to clear the dirt from his eyes. "Don't be so bloody childish, woman," he rasped, obviously not finding any humour in the situation. It appeared to make him angrier, if such a thing was possible.

Jenny tried to smother her laughter, but she could not wipe the grin off her face. She hastily turned away and scrambled as best she could from the ditch, grasping handfuls of grass and tree roots to help herself up from the soggy ground. When she reached the top, she stood and looked triumphantly down at him. "My, my, if your brothers could see you now. I'll send them back to help you, shall I?"

Darius gritted his teeth and muttered something unprintable under his breath, as he heard her peals of laughter fading into the distance.

𐌴 𐌴 𐌴 𐌴 𐌴 𐌴

When Jenny neared the house, her own amusement died as she realized she could not enter undetected, because his brothers, along with Gina and Rachel, were standing outside on the patio talking together.

"What happened?" Rachel gasped at the sight of her muddy and dripping sister, while the men tried to hide their smiles, torn between humour and concern.

"Don't ask!" Jenny said tightly, as she stamped past them shedding small clumps of mud and disappeared into the small utility room beside the kitchen.

The brothers' mirth was unrestrained, however, when a bedraggled Darius limped across the lawn towards them. Gone was the immaculate head of the company. The dishevelled man who approached them bore no resemblance to their normally well-groomed brother. They could hear his angry breathing and squelching shoes as Darius neared them, and dark clinging mud was sliding slowly from his hair, and down his clothes.

"It's not bloody funny," Darius snapped, glaring at them, daring anyone to speak as he stalked by the group and entered the house.

Gina stared after him, a mischievous smile on her face, as she called out. "Darius, don't you dare walk all that mud into the house."

He turned and gave her a withering look, said something rude and disappeared inside. Gina laughed at her brothers, who were leaning on each other, weak with laughter at the spectacle of their staid and always-in-charge brother reduced to such a state. James managed to sober up and wondered aloud what the two had been up to in the stagnant water.

"I didn't think mud wrestling was his thing," he commented, which reduced them all to further laughter.

"I'd better go and see if Jenny's all right and find out what happened," Rachel giggled up at him. She pulled away and made her way to the house.

When Rachel entered their room, Jenny was nowhere in sight, but she could hear the shower running and opened the bathroom door nearly tripping over the trail of discarded muddy clothes on the floor.

The shower door slid open, and a pink and glowing Jenny emerged, sighing. "Phew, that's better, I was absolutely plastered with mud, and it got into places that I wouldn't have thought possible."

Rachel leaned against the door frame, watching her sister as she vigorously dried herself on the large bath towel, and regarded her with an amused smile. "What did you manage to do this time, Jen? I could almost see the sparks of rage shooting from his eyes."

"Why do you automatically assume that this was my doing, and why does this keep happening?" Jenny wrapped a dressing gown around herself and threw her hands out in exasperation. "If he thought

I was a witch before, now he'll be convinced of it, and quite honestly I'm starting to wonder about that myself."

"Don't be silly, Jen," Rachel laughed softly. "Tell me what went on. We're all dying to know." After her sister explained her latest disaster, Rachel giggled. "Maybe you're right, maybe you really have put a curse on him."

"It's not really funny for him, I guess, and I must admit I had a job to curb my own amusement when he sat there all covered in mud like that," Jenny laughed. "It just struck me as hysterically funny at that moment, maybe not so much now. I can only put it down to shock at him suddenly appearing and joining me in the mud. It will just be another black mark against me to add to my lengthy list of faults. I don't think he will forget me in a hurry, do you?"

As Jenny spoke, Rachel became aware of the packed bag on the bed and shot her a questioning look. "Jen, don't you dare leave me here on my own."

"Give me a break, Rachel," her sister frowned. "I came as you asked, much against my will I might add, and all I seem to do is disrupt everything. I can't face Darius again. I feel embarrassed enough already, and they're probably all still cackling about me down there."

"I heard Gina say that he has got some sort of engagement he can't miss tonight, so you won't see him anyway." Rachel begged her to stay for at least one more night. "Please, sis, just for me. We are leaving anyway in the morning, so what will it hurt?"

"Oh, all right," Jenny's resolution wavered at the desperate plea in her sister's eyes. "But don't blame me if something else goes horribly wrong."

ꑶꑶꑶꑶꑶꑶ

That evening, Jenny relaxed, her embarrassment dispersed by the merriment and glee that Darius's brothers and sister were filled with about this latest escapade, and she found herself laughing along with them. James's older brother Dominic was two years younger than

Darius and an open easy-going man. Jenny found herself drawn to his good-humoured nature. She studied him as they talked. Such a pity, she thought, as Dominic informed her that he was engaged to someone called Samantha. Jenny would have enjoyed getting to know him better, she sensed an attraction between them that may possibly have developed into something more had he been free. As it was, he amused and entertained her. She was still smiling as Rachel and her climbed the stairs to their welcoming beds.

"Jen, I won't be in for a while," Rachel hesitated at the door. She blushed at her sister's inquiring look. "James is waiting for me. In fact, don't wait up."

Jenny nodded understandingly, hoping her sister was being careful. She sat and undressed slowly, worried about Rachel, lay back tiredly on the bed and almost instantly drifted off.

Jenny became aware that her legs felt wet, and shock made her open her eyes. She was on a strange beach and waves were lapping at her feet. She scrambled up panic-stricken. "Oh, God, where am I?" Jenny moaned. How had she come to be here? Her fear increased as she saw that her beach was little more than a low sand bank which was shrinking rapidly, and whichever direction she looked was a dark forbidding sea with a storm brewing, driving the rising water on towards her. The waves were becoming mountainous and one monstrous wave arched up and came crashing down onto where she was standing, leaving Jenny mesmerised with fear as she watched her fate approach. Jenny did not want to die, and the terrified scream that rang through the house woke everyone.

"What the hell?" Darius groaned and sat up abruptly. He could hear soft, moaning sobs echoing along the landing and he scrambled out of bed, threw his dressing gown on and raced along the corridor. His brothers were congregated around Jenny's door and Gina was putting her hand out to open it.

"Stand aside," Darius commanded, barging through the milling bodies. He pushed the door open and was confronted by the sight of Jenny, arms raised defensively, with her face white with terror and dripping with tears. Darius rushed over and sat on the bed, gathering her up into his arms, holding her firmly against his broad chest.

"It's all right, ssh, baby! I've got you. I've got you," he whispered, his hands caressing her back. Had he turned around, Darius would have seen the raised brows of his siblings as they took in the scene. Gina gave her brothers a meaningful look and they gazed back at her equally amazed. They had never seen their arrogant brother act like this, so tenderly protective. As if Darius could sense them staring, he muttered over his shoulder. "Clear off, the lot of you, I'll deal with this."

Darius heard the door quietly close and gazed down at the quivering figure in his arms, her hands were kneading through the whorls of hair on his chest like a kitten, making him aware that his robe had fallen open. He glanced down and saw that one strap of her flimsy night-dress had slipped, nearly exposing one soft full breast. He drew his breath in as he felt the rise of desire and was appalled. They were right, he was a pervert, how could he feel like this? He was supposed to rescue her from her nightmare, not imagine ravishing her. Wasn't this the woman he did not want anywhere near him? Darius gave a deep sigh. Who was he kidding? It certainly felt right.

Jenny was still leaning against his comforting warmth gratefully. She had recovered, but wasn't about to say so, because this felt so good. Jenny pressed her face against his chest and felt him shudder. She sneaked a look down, saw his problem and smiled to herself, then blushed and bit her lip as an answering and unwelcome emotion raced through her own body. This was ridiculous she thought, this can't be happening, not to us, we don't even like each other. She pulled away and gazed up at him. In turn, Darius stared down at her silently, his eyes hot with desire. She gave a faint embarrassed gasp, and lowered her own eyes before he could see her own torment.

"Well." Jenny cleared her throat nervously and gave a wobbly smile. "Thanks for the shoulder to cry on, and I am so sorry for disturbing everyone. I'll be fine now, Darius, honestly."

His arms slid away and stood up so suddenly that she nearly fell over. Darius tightened his dressing gown around him, his face flushed, made sure he was well covered and strode angrily to the door. He wrenched it open and slammed it shut behind him, without saying a single word.

Jenny stared at the door, stunned. "Now what have I done now?" she muttered. "Why is he so angry?"

ଯ ଯ ଯ ଯ ଯ ଯ

Darius was fuming, but his anger was directed more towards himself. Had he taken leave of his senses? She was the last woman on the planet he wanted to get involved with, not that she had encouraged him in any way, but still he did not want her getting any romantic ideas as far as he was concerned. So, he had felt some sort of attraction. Okay, if he must be honest, a raging desire. Probably just his hormones kicking in, and who wouldn't feel like that, holding her small, thoroughly delectable body in their arms? His imagination worked overtime, and Darius felt hot, almost feverish. He visualised other men holding Jenny like this, and his rage threatened to consume him. He stopped and put his hand to his head, horrified by his own thoughts. What was she doing to him?

"For God's sake, what are you thinking, you idiot," he muttered. "She means nothing to you. Get some control."

"My, my, she has got you rattled, hasn't she?" A prodding voice penetrated his jumbled mind. Gina was standing, arms folded, leaning casually against his bedroom door, and Darius glared at her, then shouldered her aside and slammed the door rudely in her face. She stared at it, smiling gleefully. Gina was vastly amused by the whole interlude. Her serious, arrogant brother had been reduced to a quivering wreck by a slip of a girl, and it served him right. It was about time someone got under his polished veneer. Darius needed someone to love, and Jenny was the perfect candidate. Gina hummed happily to herself as she made her way back to her bed.

Behind his closed door, her brother was pacing agitatedly about his bedroom, because he could not get that blasted woman out of his brain. As he thought of her bed, his mind suddenly registered that her sister's had been empty, Darius had been so occupied with Jenny that it had not occurred to him to wonder where Rachel was at the time. James, it seemed, would have to be given a lecture on discretion. Isabel was due home the next day, and if she thought her precious boy was getting entangled in an undesirable liaison, she would make Rachel's life hell.

༄ ༄ ༄ ༄ ༄ ༄

Jenny had been hoping to sneak away early the next morning, but Gina forestalled her. "I won't hear of you leaving at this hour, and you simply must stay until at least the evening meal. You will have plenty of time to get back. James can drive you. Besides, Isabel and father are due home, so you must meet them." Her gaze switched to Rachel. "James will expect to introduce you to his mother."

The girls stared at her questioningly. She had not referred to Isabel as my mother. Gina shook her head. "Has no one told you? Isabel is our stepmother. James is her son by my father."

"Oh, I see," Rachel said, with a nervous smile. "I hope she approves of me."

"Just remember you are the girl James has chosen, and he would not have brought you here unless he thought a great deal of you, so don't be put off by her attitude. Isabel can be quite petulant, and critical at times." Gina gave her an encouraging smile. "Just take things as they come."

༄ ༄ ༄ ༄ ༄

There was no sign of Darius throughout the day, but Jenny found herself unable to relax and kept watching the door, waiting patiently for when the time came to go home. Jenny could not face him again.

If she wasn't causing him to have an accident, she was flashing her body at him. He either thought she was mad or trying to ensnare him. She laughed at her own thoughts; he was probably glad of the excuse to leave the house and get away from her. If she closed her eyes, Jenny could still feel the firm, well-muscled body that she had been held against, could still visualise the hairy tanned chest. Then as her wayward mind travelled downwards, she felt the heat moving in her and gave an exasperated sigh at her own weak stupidity. She mentally berated herself for dwelling on him like this. Time to occupy myself with something else, I think, she told herself.

Jenny was leaning back in a comfortable chair reading an interesting book from the study, when a commotion at the door made her glance up. The striking woman who entered was obviously Isabel. Her head was thrown back and she was laughing up at the blond, attractive man beside her. Was this Darius's father?

As Isabel swept in, she brought a small group of people with her, all immaculately dressed, as if they were ready for a party. A darkly handsome older man followed them. He was so like Darius that her heart jumped with shock, and conjecture that any other man could be his father was quickly dispelled. The photograph in the study must be of this man.

My goodness, Jenny thought, if Darius aged as well as his father, he would be even more imposing than he already was. The older man carried more weight, yet was still trim and upright. She could see where the brothers got their stature from, and their swarthy good looks.

Rachel was nervous as she was introduced to James's parents and he kept his arm protectively around her, a fact that Isabel noted with disapproval, and her lips tightened ominously. Her hand barely touched Rachel's, and her murmured greeting was lost, as she turned away, beginning an animated conversation with one of her friends.

Jenny moved protectively towards Rachel as she saw the flush of embarrassment on her sister's face. She felt absolutely livid at this deliberate snub, but James was already guiding Rachel solicitously towards one of the couches, his face set in lines of hard anger which denoted trouble for his mother later. His father's face was equally tight, and he apologised for his wife's behaviour, excusing her on the grounds that she was just tired from their journey. He made an effort to relax and smiled at both girls.

"As you may have surmised, I am Charles Langston, and I am very pleased to meet you both. Any friends of James are most welcome here. Now you girls go and enjoy yourselves, this is supposed to be a party." Then he turned and made his way to his wife's side, with a determined expression.

James was left staring after his father with frustration, not having had the chance of explaining exactly how much Rachel meant to him.

Jenny looked around with vexation for Gina, who caught her eye and tried to sidle away as she approached.

"No, you don't. Why didn't you tell us that this was another party." Jenny hissed. "At least we could have dressed accordingly."

"You both look perfectly presentable to me," Gina eyed her up and down. "And anyway, you wouldn't have stayed if I had told you about it, now would you?"

"Dead right I wouldn't, especially if I'd known how rude your stepmother was going to be to Rachel." Jenny glared at her in exasperation.

Gina glanced across at Isabel holding court in the middle of the room, and her face became cold. "Her endless capacity for bad manners surprises even me at times." She shrugged and turned back to Jenny. Gina indicated the graceful, dark-haired girl hovering beside her stepmother. "She's probably going on about what a good catch Melissa is for Darius. It gets rather repetitive."

Jenny sensed a deep dislike running through the family as she looked around at the various expressions of distaste on their faces. Even James, whose mother Isabel was, looked embarrassed and angry.

Suddenly she wanted to leave this house and its underlying tension. These were not her kind of people.

The meal and party dragged on interminably and Jenny found herself casting furtive glances at her wristwatch. She shook it, certain it had stopped.

"Are we boring you my dear?" a voice chimed sarcastically.

"Not at all, Mrs Langston." Jenny hastily lifted her head, pasting a polite smile on her face. "I am just a little tired, that's all."

Isabel stared at her with cold blue eyes, then gave a small icy smile. "I hear that you and your sister run a little 'second-hand shop,' I believe it's called." Isabel made it sound like a disease, the way she emphasised the words. She looked questioningly at Jenny, who sensed danger from this haughty woman.

"Yes, that's right," Jenny answered quietly, waiting for the next put-down. It wasn't long in coming.

"And what sort of people shop there, my dear, down and outs?" Isabel glanced around at her cronies and gave a mocking snigger.

"As it happens, no, Mrs Langston. There are some people who have had an unfortunate life and can't afford much. The odd item or two does go missing, but they are still welcome to browse around my shop. Most people I find are very pleasant to talk to, and most people are honest. You'd be surprised at some of my clientele." Jenny gazed at her with narrowed eyes. She paused and added. "There are not many people that I dislike on sight, but there's always the odd one who crops up, of course!" Jenny smiled politely and turned away, hearing the other women guests titter as she did so. She would not give Isabel the satisfaction of seeing her anger.

Isabel had a smile on her lips, but they were tight and her eyes blazed. How dare that dreadful girl look at her like that. She would not allow James to mix with such undesirables.

Jenny found Rachel sitting alone. "Odious woman," she snapped.

"Who, me?" her sister queried with a smile.

"No, that awful Isabel," Jenny laughed.

Rachel looked across the room and saw the woman in question, staring coldly back at them. She shivered and hastily averted her gaze. "Oh, Jen, she's glaring daggers at us. What on earth did she say?" Her sister told her about Isabel's unfriendly and insulting attitude towards her, and Rachel sighed. "I knew she didn't like us, I just felt it when I first saw her enter here tonight. I think she wants James to find someone a lot more acceptable." She glanced around the room as if seeking his comfort.

Jenny followed her gaze. "Where is James anyway?"

"Oh, Darius called. Apparently, his car has broken down and James volunteered to rescue him," her sister answered.

Jenny felt annoyed. She would have spent the day in a far more relaxed mood if she had known Darius was away from the house. Rachel's small moan of distress made her glance searchingly around. James had just entered, and on his arm was the beautiful red-haired girl who had wrapped herself around him on the terrace the previous day. She was gazing up at him with a flirtatious expression and laughing, her mouth parting as he bent his head and kissed her tenderly on the lips. As both girls stared across at him in shock at his blatant flirting, he raised his eyes and stared straight through them, causing Rachel to gasp as though she was in pain.

"I can't stay here, Jen," she whispered, leaping up and clutching at Jenny's arm. "I just can't. Let's go home, please."

Her eyes were swimming with tears and Jenny knew that her sister was hanging on to her dignity by a thread. Jenny felt so angry with James for ignoring them that, had he spoken to them right at that moment, she would willingly have struck him. How dare he play games with her sister? It was probably the way his sort got their fun. She gazed at the gathering with disgust. They were welcome to each other. She knew Rachel's misery could not be contained for much longer, so Jenny slipped one arm through her sister's, gently, guiding her unobtrusively from the room and up the stairs.

The girls packed quickly and quietly. No conversation passed between them. One word would have made Rachel break down. Jenny glanced anxiously at her sister from time to time, her white face and silent tears tore at her heart, and she felt nothing but contempt for the perpetrator of such misery. Nobody saw them leave. Jenny had called a taxi, and it was waiting at the end of the drive for them. As the vehicle pulled away, Jenny put her arm around her stricken sister and glanced back with angry eyes at the large house. The lights were blazing, and the party was still in full swing, it looked deceptively welcoming in its tranquil setting. Yet underneath, a deep unhappiness pervaded the atmosphere. Jenny shivered, glad to leave the place behind.

פ פ פ פ פ פ

During the following days, Jenny began to pay Rachel closer attention. Her red swollen eyes and constant crying bouts were a cause for concern, and she felt at a loss. How could she console her? What could Jenny say that would be of any use in comforting her sister? The truth was Rachel had fallen for a two-timing snake and nothing Jenny could say was going to alter that fact.

Rachel moped about the flat, jumping every time the phone rang, looking longingly at it, but refusing to take any calls from James. Even when Gina called, she would not speak to her. Jenny felt much the same, giving any of the brothers short shrift when they tried to explain. Rachel had not shown her face in the shop for three weeks, which made life a bit hectic for Jenny, who was trying to juggle her designs with running the business. As her sister was not going to be of much use for a while, Jenny persuaded her that it might be an ideal time to go and stay in Scotland with their parents.

"Just for a short time, sis, until you feel more able to handle this unfortunate episode." She held Rachel's hand and added as her sister shook her head, "Please, Rachel, think about it. You need to get away from here, to take a breather even if only for a few days. Go to mum. You need a chance to get over what happened and decide what to do about James. Either face him or walk away. Your choice."

Two more miserable days passed, and then Rachel suddenly made her mind up. "I will go, you're right, Jen, I need to leave here for a while to sort my head out."

Her sister packed and left that same day. Her mother had told her to come up immediately, and Rachel had taken her at her word.

Chapter Seven

The flat seemed so quiet and empty without Rachel that Jenny found herself feeling restless. She was unused to living alone, so she began to spend far more of her time in the evenings down in her small workroom. One evening after she had closed the shop, Jenny did not even bother going upstairs. She headed once again for her drawing board.

"Just an hour, then I'll go get something to eat," she promised herself. She had been working for an hour and a half when she heard the door rattle, and someone tapped on the window. "Drat," she muttered. It was sure to be Jason, and she really did not feel like being bothered by him at this moment, so Jenny ignored it and went on with her designing. The tapping became more persistent, and she sighed with irritation, jumped up and marched purposefully through to the front of the shop.

Jenny peered through the glass, and she was jolted to see not Jason, but James smiling hesitantly at her. She wrenched the door open, glaring up at him belligerently.

"I wasn't going to open the door when I realised who it was, but I could not resist this chance of telling you what I think of you! You two-timing pig."

"I'm not James." The young man held his hands up placatingly, cutting across her angry words.

"Pardon?" Jenny stopped mid-tirade, then said sarcastically. "Wow, you could have fooled me. What is this, some new ploy to pretend you have morphed overnight into a nice guy?"

"I am nice, I hope. I'm Jake, his twin." He smiled down at her and laughed at her shocked face. "Your mouth is open."

Jenny clamped it shut and rubbed her hands over her tired face. She stared up at him. "This is too surreal to be a joke. I think you'd better come up to the flat and explain. Just let me close up and turn the lights off."

Jake sat and watched Jenny as she busied herself making coffee. She was quite vibrant and pretty, it was no wonder that James loved her. "You would not return James's calls and when he did turn up, you wouldn't even open the door. He is totally devastated. My poor brother doesn't even know what he's supposed to have done."

Jenny snorted in disbelief, then stood with the tray in her hands looking down at him, with a growing frown. Twins! Was that the simple answer? An easy mistake to make. Jenny smiled as she realised he had also made a mistake. He was obviously confusing her with her sister. She pointed out that Rachel, seeing him with his girlfriend, had made the forgivable error of assuming he was James. As Jenny talked and explained the awful mistake, his eyes widened. It became apparent that he himself had also made one.

"I'm sorry," Jake said. "I thought you were Rachel."

They stared at each other and laughed in amusement. Jenny felt elated, then guilty. She herself had been too ready to condemn. "How come we never saw the two of you together?" Jenny gave him a puzzled frown.

"I was away when Rachel met the family, and it was pure coincidence that James had been called away at one point during the evening. We must have kept missing each other, yet you obviously would only see one of us and assume it was the same person. No wonder Rachel thought he was two-timing her. Yet surely she must have thought it a bit blatant of him to parade another girl in front of her? What a shambles this has turned out to be," he said, apologetically.

"I think Rachel could be forgiven for jumping to conclusions. After all, seeing you kiss your girlfriend would have overridden any rational thought at that particular moment. I will give Rachel a ring and try and put things straight," she said, jumping to her feet.

Nobody had thought about telling them that James had a twin, and she wondered about that. Why didn't James himself mention it? As she went to pick the phone up, Jake forestalled her. "I have a better idea, Jenny. Why don't James and I travel up to Scotland and visit your parents' home? I have contacts up there, so I can conduct business while James tries to straighten things out with Rachel. When she sees the two of us together, she must believe him, mustn't she?"

Jenny was pleased and thought it was a great idea. When Rachel hurt, so did she. What better way was there to clear things up than to see the two men together right in front of her? No doubt their mother was a great comfort to her sister, and Rachel could not have sought refuge in a better place, but James was the only tonic that could cure what ailed her.

When Jake left, Jenny sat at the table with her evening meal, toying with the food, her head propped up on one hand deep in thought. Part of her missed Darius, and to her dismay, he was taking over her mind. She found herself remembering the tanned expanse of muscular chest as he had held her against him, the powerful thighs she had glimpsed through the gap in his robe, then Jenny felt hot as she recalled what else she had seen. This simply had to stop. Jenny thought of him too often for comfort, even when she lay in bed at night, she wondered what he was doing, where he was, who with. She felt a surge of jealousy, which was stupid because he had most certainly already pushed her out of his mind by now. Jenny sighed miserably and decided on an early night.

The man in question was having way too many sleepless nights for his liking and when he did sleep, his brothers had to keep leading him back to his bed. Apparently, much to his mortification and his brothers' amusement, Darius kept climbing into the single bed in the pretty little guest room and the pillow was clutched so tightly in his arms that they had a job to prize it away from him. At breakfast, his father glanced at him over the top of his paper, rustling it in irritation. "What the devil is wrong with you these days, Darius? Are you overdoing things at work, taking on too much, is that it?"

He could feel his brothers' eyes fixed on him, waiting with great interest for his reply. They smirked at each other as he answered. "I've got an irritating problem on my mind."

"Some work problem, is it that damn Sanderson?" His father set his paper down. "I said he would try and wriggle out of the deal."

"It's nothing to do with work, Dad." Darius shook his head. 'Everything is absolutely fine in that respect.'

"Would the irritating problem have a name?" Dominic grinned at him.

"No! She would not," Darius said, glaring balefully at him.

"She?" His brother's grin widened. Whatever Darius had been about to retaliate was left unsaid, as Isabel sauntered into the room, and sat down.

"Good morning, darlings. Which woman are you referring to? I do hope you mean Melissa."

"Who I see or don't see is nothing at all to do with you, Isabel," Darius said in a low clipped voice and stood up with a face like thunder. Then he thrust his chair noisily back under the table and strode from the room, letting the door bang behind him. The others stared after him in various stages of shock, this was not like their cool and collected brother, such touchiness was completely out of character. Gina gazed after him speculatively. Could her brother really have been snared at last, as she had speculated? Their father gave a bark of laughter as he met her knowing look and shook his head warningly at her.

"Let him work it out for himself, Gina."

"Well!" Isabel huffed crossly. "Why do you let him talk to me in that way, Charles?" She glared at her husband, who was regarding her with a strange expression on his face, one that appeared to be a permanent fixture these days whenever he saw her.

"You bring it on yourself, my dear," he drawled. "He is a grown man, and I am sure that if Darius wants your advice, he will ask for it." Then he flicked his paper crisply and raised it up again, ignoring her.

Isabel seethed as she nibbled at her food, looking around the table at her stepchildren. They had never taken to her, she knew that. Oh, she had tried to make them like her at first, but it seemed that no matter what she did, Isabel could never make any headway with them. She could not measure up to their dead mother. It did not occur to her that it might be her own selfish and intolerant nature which pushed people away. Isabel sat up straight as she realised that her own two sons were missing from the table. "Where are James and Jake?" she asked. The conversation at the table died, and she had their momentary attention, but nobody bothered to answer. "Well?" she demanded, her voice rising.

Charles sighed impatiently and lowered his paper. "I believe they have some important business to deal with in Scotland," he said, tersely. With that he turned his eyes once more to his paper and the family resumed their conversation.

Isabel sat feeling snubbed and hurt. This was becoming a habit, she thought bitterly. Part of her trouble was that she had always been jealous of the close bond between her husband and his first family. Isabel also knew that he would never love her with the same depth of feeling he had harboured for his first wife. It was something she could not fight, even giving Charles two more children had not bought her the place in their affections that she craved. Instead of maturing into her role, Isabel had simply gone out of her way to behave even more childishly, which had caused the whole situation to become worse. Now she and her husband hardly communicated anymore.

Charles had been a lonely man when she had first met him. Isabel had been so in love with him that she had thought to trap him into marriage by becoming pregnant, and it had worked. She had lived to regret her stupidity. Over the years. an invisible barrier had grown between them and her own selfish nature had compounded it, yet within her a measure of love still struggled to survive. Isabel just had no idea about how to lower her side of the divide. As a result, she was lonely and now it seemed that James and Jake were going to transfer their love to someone else, as well, and it was not in her nature to share.

Isabel had reluctantly put up with Lauren, Jake's fiancée, because of her family. They were what Isabel regarded as socially acceptable. What she could not tolerate was James's latest unfortunate choice. Something would have to be done about that.

At that moment, James's unfortunate choice was held close against his heart, crying with relief and guilt at having doubted him.

ꀤ ꀤ ꀤ ꀤ ꀤ ꀤ

When James and his brother arrived in Scotland, they had booked themselves into a hotel close to Rachel's parents' house. Now they were preparing to go and visit Rachel, and James was naturally apprehensive about seeing her.

"Suppose she thinks that we were playing a joke? Rachel won't be very amused, will she?" He sank down onto his bed, rubbing his hands together nervously.

"For Pete's sake, James, why should she think anything of the sort?"

"Oh, come on, Jake, how many times have we tried to confuse people in the past?" James laughed sadly. "All very funny at the time, but I don't find it quite so amusing now."

Jake lounged against the door, hands in his pockets, regarding his brother with ill-concealed impatience. "Why the heck didn't you tell her about me? Am I some dark secret or something?"

"Sorry, Jake. I just wanted to be me; you know, liked for myself. You always could pull the girls. They seem to gravitate towards you." James shrugged unhappily and he added, quietly, looking down at his hands, "I love Rachel so much, Jake, and I didn't want to lose her to you."

Jake straightened up from his lounging position, and took his hands out of his pockets, feeling a sense of shock. He walked over and placed his hand lightly on his brother's shoulder. "James, you fool, I would never, and I mean never, try for any girl you were serious about, and if Rachel really loves you, she won't even look at me."

"She can't help looking at you," James stated, with a hopeless shrug. "You are me. How is Rachel supposed to tell the difference?"

"Have some faith in yourself and her. She will know." Jake shook him impatiently.

James just nodded but could not bring himself to really believe it. He looked at his brother enviously. Jake was completely unaware of his own charm. Women would see the two of them together, then gradually their interest in James would wane and be transferred to Jake, so he had found it easier never to introduce girls to his brother. In fact, James never made mention that he was a twin. He just wished he possessed half the confidence that gave his brother such a charismatic presence.

When they arrived at the house, James stood with his heart in his mouth, waiting for the door to open. The attractive grey-haired woman who stood in the entrance eyed him sternly. "You are James, I take it?"

"How did you know?" he said. James was taken aback and glanced sideways at Jake.

"You're the guilty looking one," she said with a smile. "Come on, you had better come in. You've got some bridges to mend, my lad."

Rachel's mother showed them into a cosy living room and told them that Rachel would be in shortly. Jenny had telephoned her mother in advance and apprised her of the situation before the brothers left on their journey. Her mother was relieved to know that Rachel's disillusionment was misplaced. Her daughter had been so upset, and like Jenny, her mother suffered for her. Nothing hurt more than seeing their child break down. It eased her mind when Jenny called and informed her that it had all been caused by a misunderstanding, so she was looking forward to meeting with these two young men. In the meantime, she promised Jenny that she would explain the mistake to Rachel. James would have to be the one who had to explain to Rachel as to why he had thought fit to keep his brother a secret.

They heard the front door slam and then Rachel came slowly into the room. She stared at the two tall men who stood regarding her with apprehension, and her eyes rounded in bewilderment.

"My God! You are so alike. James, why didn't you tell me that you had an identical twin? Didn't it occur to you that I might think the worst when I saw your brother with his girlfriend?" she gasped. Rachel sat down abruptly holding her hands to her cheeks. "This is such a shock. I just can't get over it."

James had not spoken. He was waiting with a feeling of dread to see who Rachel picked. The sensible part of him knew that it would be difficult for anyone to tell them apart. The part that was desperately in love wanted her to sense that love in him.

Rachel got to her feet and walked across to them. Both men looked down at her with identical smiles. She stared carefully at them and then without hesitation veered towards James. Only one man's eyes held anxiety and love. Rachel put her hands on his chest. "Oh, James, did you think that I wouldn't know you? I love you too much not to." Then she put her hands over her eyes and burst into tears. "I should have trusted you. How could I have thought you would do something so hurtful?"

Jake watched them with a lump in his throat. He had hated to see his brother so down, and now their obvious happiness and love for each other gave him a twinge of envy. He could only hope that his girlfriend, Lauren, harboured the same depth of feeling for him as Rachel had for James.

Jake thought this might be a good time to make himself scarce and slipped quietly out of the room to cadge a cup of tea off Rachel's mother. His departure went totally unnoticed by the two people clinging onto each other desperately.

James stood hugging Rachel tightly to him, his chest swelling with love for her. "Don't cry, Rachel, please don't. Do you forgive me for being so stupid?" James raised her face and lowered his head to meet her willing lips. There was no further need for words.

After an hour had passed, Jake decided to take a quick peek at the love birds. He peered into the room and winked as he caught his brother's eye. James mouthed at him to clear off, and his brother melted away with a satisfied grin on his face. Another cup of tea was in order, and a progress report on the situation for her parents.

Rachel was so happy spending this time with James that she did not want to leave. She was frightened that when things got back to normal, something else would get in the way of their happiness, and when the time came to go, she hugged her parents tearfully. "I have missed you two, I didn't realise quite how much until I saw you again."

"There, look what you have done to my shirt, I'm soaked! Now I'll have to wring it out after you've gone," her father said gruffly, patting her back affectionately.

Rachel gave a tearful laugh and wiped her eyes, as she looked into his familiar smiling face. "I won't leave it so long next time," she promised.

Seeing the closeness of Rachel's parents had been a revelation for both men. They seemed so happy and content with their lot, and the humorous repartee between the older couple made the visit relaxing and pleasant. They could not help but compare them with their own parents' relationship, which seemed sadly lacking in warmth. Rachel was flanked by the two tall brothers as they waved goodbye to her parents.

"My goodness, they are strapping boys. Good-looking, too," her mother said quietly to her husband.

"They make a nice couple, I must say." He smiled with pride and waved at his pretty daughter as the three young people piled into Jake's car. "Let's hope nothing else happens to spoil things for Rachel."

He squeezed his wife's waist as they waved goodbye, then turned and went back inside the house. They had always hoped that the girls would have the good fortune to find the sort of love that they shared, and maybe Rachel had, which just left Jenny, the quiet one.

༄ ༄ ༄ ༄ ༄ ༄

The quiet one was, at that moment, gnashing her teeth and muttering words to herself that would have made her mother's straight hair curl if she had heard them. The reason was Jason, who was once more making a nuisance of himself, and he just would not take no for an answer.

"Please, just this once. No strings, I promise." Jason flushed and cleared his throat. "As a matter of fact, I want to ask your advice about a girl I've recently met." Jenny's anger abated and she stared at him in surprise. He flushed even more at the wary look on her face. "I know I've been a bit of a nuisance, and also that I was wasting my time. I guess I was just lonely, and you are a very nice girl, Jenny." He smiled at her. "I really was smitten, you know, or thought I was."

"Until you met this other girl." Jenny smiled up at him with evident relief at this welcome news.

"Yes, I've never felt like this before," he laughed. "So, will you come for a meal with me, simply as friends?"

She studied him, hoping this wasn't some sort of ploy, yet he appeared to be serious, and she was hungry, so why not take up his offer? "Yes, I would like to share a meal with you, Jason, purely as a friend," Jenny stipulated, giving him a straight look.

He looked so taken aback, that she laughed. Jason obviously thought that it would have taken much more persuasion for her to accept his invitation. "Great," he said, with a pleased expression. "I'll pick you up in an hour."

When Jason named the place in town where they were to dine, her eyebrows shot up. My goodness, they would be eating in exalted company tonight, she thought. "Why there?" Jenny queried.

"Why not," he replied, then added. "As it happens, I've had a few good sales this week, so money is no object, and as a matter of fact, I have seen this girl there before."

"Ah, I see," Jenny nodded. "And does she have a name, would I know her?"

"I doubt it very much, she doesn't come from around this district. Anyway, I'll see you later," Jason said quickly. Then with a brief wave, he was off.

Jenny rifled through her clothes wondering what on earth she could wear, as her choice was extremely limited. In the end, she gave up, went into Rachel's room, and rummaged through the selection of pretty dresses that packed her sister's wardrobe. Jenny's eye was drawn to a shimmering green dress. It reminded her of a deep pool, sparkling in the sunlight. She held it up and gazed at herself in the mirror with an arrested expression, surprised and pleased by her own reflection. The colour did wonderful things for her hair and skin and matched her glowing eyes. In fact, Jenny thought, I look darned attractive. The dress was slightly longer on her than it would have been on her sister, but everywhere else fit perfectly.

Jason rang the bell and waited patiently for the door to open. He was awed by the vision of loveliness that confronted him when it finally did, and she smiled up at him.

"Wow! You look terrific," he breathed.

"I know," Jenny laughed happily. Her laughter died at the warm look in his eyes.

"It's okay." Jason smiled wryly at her wary expression. "This is purely a look of lustful appreciation. My thoughts are elsewhere."

She was not entirely convinced, but Jenny took the proffered arm as he guided her along the dark gravel path to his car. It was a long time since Jenny had been taken out and treated to a meal. Her work was time-consuming, and she was determined to enjoy this evening off.

The restaurant consisted of two floors, with most of the tables set out into small niches, interspersed with stands of foliage strategically placed to give the utmost privacy to the diners, and Jenny felt excited as Jason escorted her over to the lift.

"Nothing but the best, my dear girl. We shall eat upstairs this evening. You get a lovely view of the river from up there, and with all the lights reflected in the water, it's quite a remarkable sight to behold." He smiled at her, as she gazed around at the beautiful decor. "Impressed?"

"Who wouldn't be? This place has been so tastefully designed," Jenny said, as she returned his smile with a wary one of her own. She was getting an odd feeling that all was not as it appeared, but Jenny decided to make the most of her meal and see what followed at the end of the evening.

Jason chuckled. He glanced around him with growing confidence as he watched Jenny's sparkling eyes. If nothing else, he had brought pleasure to his heart's desire. All he had to do now was show her what a good prospective partner he would make.

Jenny knew she looked her best and was aware that she had attracted a good amount of interested glances as Jason led her to their table. The atmosphere made her feel relaxed and comfortable. The discrete seating and soft lights only adding to her feeling of content. Jenny sat watching the surrounds of the restaurant that she could see from her secluded seat, her eyes scanning the beautifully dressed people who gradually filled the room. The food when placed in front of them looked exquisite and tasted just as delicious as the aroma had promised.

Jenny tucked in hungrily, and was just enjoying her second mouthful when her fork stopped midair and her eyes rounded. Her enjoyment in the food rapidly diminished and Jenny froze in horror, her heart plummeting as she spotted Darius at one of the other tables.

She was relieved to see that he was sideways on to her, so she was not in his direct line of vision. Her relief evaporated, however, as Darius turned his head to acknowledge an acquaintance. She put her hand up to the side of her face and hoped he had not seen her. Jenny sneaked a sideways look through her fingers, and by the rigid set of his body and his fixed gaze, knew that her hopes were in vain.

Darius had not particularly wanted to go out, but Gina as usual had cajoled and pleaded until, like a fool, he had given in. He glanced uninterestedly around and caught sight of one of his business acquaintances. Darius nodded his head politely at the man, then his gaze was arrested by a pair of green eyes gleaming at him, through what she thought were shielding fingers. He gave a faint huff of laughter, which died in his throat as Darius caught sight of her male companion. A surge of uncontrollable rage coursed through him, and he had the urge to crush the man between his large hands. In fact, he had a primitive desire to pick him up and throw him through the window into the river outside. His companion leaned forward to see more clearly who had arrested his attention, because Darius looked positively murderous.

Jenny, watching, felt her heart sink even lower as she saw that it was Gina, who would be bound to try and speak to her. She felt trapped. Then her heart jumped as she saw Darius push his chair back and stand up. Jenny leaned forward and whispered frantically to Jason. "Can we go? I am so sorry, but I seem to have suddenly developed the most awful headache."

"We've still got the desert to come, and we haven't even had a chance to talk yet." Jason stared at her in consternation. His well-laid plans were unravelling in front of his eyes.

"Oh, lord," Jenny gasped, as her eyes caught the direction Darius was headed in. "Look as though you are hanging on to my every word and hold my other hand," Jenny hissed, grabbing the hand he had resting on the table.

"Pardon?" he said, startled. His voice trailed off, as he looked up at the large man with murderous black eyes, who was now looming over him. Jason tried to let go of Jenny's vice-like grip, but to no avail.

She was gazing up at the man trying to smile. "Well, fancy meeting you here, Darius. We are having such a lovely time, aren't we, darling," she said, squeezing Jason's hand even tighter.

"What? Oh! Yes, lovely place," he stammered.

Gina strolled over and stood beside her brother, glancing at him. He looked as though he were carved out of stone, Darius had not spoken, and he hadn't moved. "Well, isn't this a nice coincidence! Why not join us at our table," Gina said lightly, adding, as she saw Jenny's slight frantic shake of the head, "Oh, please do."

Jenny sat down at their table and shivered when she felt Darius's fingers touch her arms, as he guided her into her seat.

Darius sat staring at the untouched food on his plate. He had felt Jenny's shiver of revulsion as he touched her, and his heart was heavy with what he saw as her rejection. His introspection was interrupted by Gina's voice.

"Isn't it, Darius?"

"Pardon?" His head jerked up.

"I said isn't it strange that we should meet them here?" She gave him an amused smile. "We don't come here very often, do we?"

Darius did not reply. His eyes were fixated on the other couple's entwined hands, and the rage on his face was awesome to behold.

Jason swallowed nervously. "Do you mind if we leave now, Jenny, I seem to have caught your headache." He laughed weakly, then stopped abruptly as he looked at Darius, whose black eyes were regarding him coldly and his hands were flexing as though he would like to strangle him.

"Oh, you poor, poor thing," Jenny cooed, jumping up with alacrity and touching Jason's forehead lovingly with her hand. She pulled him to his feet. "Let's get you home, darling."

She smiled emptily at Gina, avoiding Darius's furious eyes, and thanked her for inviting them to her table. "Pity we could not have stayed longer. Maybe another time." Then she turned and propelled the bemused Jason rapidly from the room.

***

"Phew! What was that all about?" he asked, mopping his brow. He looked at her accusingly. "I think the man really would have killed me, you know. Is he the reason that you would not go out with me?"

"No, Jason. I didn't even know that man existed when I first met you," Jenny sighed despondently. "He only came into my life recently."

The way her eyes clouded as she spoke made him look more closely at Jenny, and his heart sank. "You love him, don't you?"

"I can't deny it, not that it will do me much good. He is way out of my league. Besides, his mother hates me, and his family think that I'm some sort of witch." Jenny shrugged hopelessly. She saw his confused face. "Never mind, it's a long story, and anyway he's spoken for."

"Then why did he look as though he would like to tear my head off? Seems to me he was as mad as hell. If that's not jealousy, then I don't know what is," Jason said, looking puzzled.

"I didn't say that he didn't want me, he just doesn't love me." Jenny gave a hollow laugh.

"It's a bit unfair on his girlfriend to act like that. Although, I must say, she was very laid back about the scene he made." Jason shook his head. This was all beyond him.

At first, Jenny looked puzzled by his words, and then understanding dawned. "Oh! Gina's not his girlfriend; she's his sister. I am so sorry, Jason, we didn't even have time to make formal introductions, did we, and this has ruined your entire evening. All that beautifully cooked meal wasted. I only managed to eat half of mine."

"His sister, you say. Extremely attractive woman, isn't she?" Jason had a faraway look in his eyes. He came down to earth as her words sank in. "Oh, don't worry about me, Jenny. I nearly cleared my plate, so at least one of us had time to enjoy the meal. No one can claim that it was not entertaining for the other diners, with all that drama playing out between you two. Perhaps we can go somewhere more local next time, not so exclusive."

"Next time? Well, why not." She stared at him, narrowing her eyes. "You never did get around to telling me about this mystery girl, did you?"

He looked sheepish and Jenny realised that there was no other woman. Although, if his interest in Gina was anything to go by, she suspected that there soon would be if he had his way, but she had a feeling that Gina was more discerning where men were concerned. She could only wish Jason luck with his efforts.

ロ ロ ロ ロ ロ ロ

Darius had leapt to his feet as Jenny had hastened from the room and stood looking venomously at the departing figure of Jason. Gina stood up and laid a restraining hand on his arm. She could feel the tension in his taut muscles.

"Murder is still a punishable offence, you know," she murmured softly.

"What?" he snapped rudely.

"Hush, Darius, lower your voice and sit down. We're attracting undue attention."

He glanced around and glared at the hastily averted faces. "They should mind their own bloody business then, shouldn't they," he growled, but nevertheless sank back down into his chair.

"Darius!" Gina hissed, warningly.

"I don't know what's wrong with me," he groaned, rubbing the back of his neck.

"Don't you," she said quietly. "Just how much are you attracted to Jenny? Do you love her, Darius?"

"Don't be so damn stupid," he snarled.

Gina smiled to herself. That had certainly touched a nerve.

Darius abruptly pushed his chair back and stood up. "This food tastes like sawdust. Let's go."

Gina watched her brother as he first helped seat her in the car and then stalked around to the other side, his rage palpable. Darius looked as though his bottled-up anger would explode at any moment. As if to prove her point, he suddenly crashed his fist violently against the roof of the car, making her jump. Gina was glad they had driven here in his car. At least it wasn't her vehicle he was denting.

"Sorry," he mumbled in a muffled voice, as he climbed in looking suitably contrite. "She seems to bring out the beast in me."

Gina hid her smile. I'll say, she thought.

Darius did not start the engine straight away. He sat gripping the steering wheel until his knuckles turned white. "She can't stand me," he said abruptly. The anguish in her brother's voice cut his sister to the heart, and she squeezed his hand.

"Oh! Darius, that is simply not true. I think it can only be because Jenny feels so attracted to you that she is running away. Her feelings frighten her."

He shook his head. "No! You didn't see the way she flinched when I touched her, and who the hell is he? She seemed to be all over him."

"For heaven's sake, Darius, I saw her eyes, you didn't. Haven't you ever shivered with pleasure? Trust me, women know these things." Gina gave him an exasperated look. Her eyes sparkled at him, and he felt a dawning hope as she went on. "Besides, that is entirely an act, she told me all about Jason. He was becoming an utter nuisance, and she could not get rid of him, there is nothing serious between them at all."

"Why does she go out with him then, and how many other men are there in the wings that I don't know about?" He stared at her, accusingly.

"Darius, will you stop putting imaginary obstacles in the way," she sighed, in exasperation.

"Do you think I should go and see her?"

"Why not?" His sister nodded. "What can you lose?"

He gazed at her, my last hope and my mind, Darius thought to himself.

ꉈ ꉈ ꉈ ꉈ ꉈ ꉈ

Jenny let herself into the flat, and to her own consternation, burst into tears, then collapsed onto the couch and cried noisily and at length. She was not even sure why. Stop being so dense, she told herself. Admit it, you love the man. He is unbalancing you, making you act like an idiot. Unrequited love can do that to you, I suppose, she thought despondently. Jenny dragged herself up and gazed into the mirror. Her swollen eyes and red nose shone back at her, and she gave a wobbly smile. "My God, he wouldn't want you if he could see you now," she murmured.

Then Jenny jumped and gave a strangled scream as a voice said huskily, "Yes, he would." and she saw his reflected face behind her in the mirror.

She whirled around breathlessly, aware of her blotchy face. "How did you get in?" Jenny demanded shakily.

"You really should make sure that your door is securely shut. You never know who might walk in," Darius said as he advanced towards her. He gazed down at her shaking figure, seeing the answering desire in Jenny's eyes before she could hide it, as she backed away. Any speech Darius may have rehearsed completely went out of his head, words failing him and he reached out for her as his need overwhelmed him.

Jenny put her hands out as though to stop him, but her arms folded uselessly as he gathered her up against him and she sagged weakly, leaning onto his large comforting body.

"Don't," she said feebly, making no effort to free herself as his head descended and his mouth sought hers. As his lips parted hers, Jenny's heart pounded so hard that it almost hurt, and she was engulfed with the overwhelming feelings his passion awoke in her. Darius's hands were moving over her, pressing her more firmly against him as his desire increased. She moaned, as his hands gripped her buttocks, manoeuvring her into a more intimate position and she felt his arousal. Then her senses almost left her as she felt the instinctive movement of his body against hers.

Panic swept through her. This must not happen. It might satisfy his sexual desire, but where did that leave her? Jenny felt him starting to grind hard against her and she knew that it would soon be beyond the point when Darius would be able to stop. Already his hands were feverishly pulling at the hem of her dress and sliding it up.

"No! No, don't make me do something we will both regret." Jenny pulled violently away from him, pushing at him frantically. She repeated his name, and he shook his head dazedly. His arms slackened and Darius flushed, as he became aware of what he was about to do. Jenny felt his body tremble against hers as he tried to control his clamouring senses.

"Why?" he groaned, reluctantly letting his arms slide away.

Jenny stood watching him as he tried to adjust his clothing to accommodate his still-aroused body, and blushed as she saw the state he was in. Darius saw her eyes fixed on him and gave a harsh laugh. "See what you do to me."

"Darius, it's pretty obvious that you want me, and I am very attracted to you, but it's not enough, not for me. I'm not looking for that sort of relationship. There has to be more to it than just hopping into bed to gain sexual relief." Jenny put her hands up to her hot cheeks, asking, as she gazed up into his set frustrated face, "Do you love me, Darius?"

"Is that an ultimatum," he snarled. His mouth set in a grim line of frustration, and his eyes narrowed. "Will you sleep with me if I say I love you and want to marry you?"

"No! We would both have to be in love for me to do that," she snapped, as her own temper rose at his hurtful words. Her anger died as quickly as it had arisen, and she felt drained. She shook her head sadly. As much as she had wanted this, it was not the way to go. His words had reduced it to nothing but a meaningless coupling. "Please go, Darius, and don't bother to come back."

Without saying another word, Darius brushed past her and walked quietly out of the door, and out of her life.

Chapter Eight

Gina was feeling fed up with her brother's boorish behaviour and resolved to do something about it. If he was not staring into space, Darius was either slamming doors or bawling them out for the smallest things, and it was driving them all mad. He had clashed with Isabel more than once, and even his father was moved to defend her from him.

"That is quite enough, Darius," his father snapped. "Get a hold of yourself, sort out whatever it is that's eating you, or clear off and find somewhere else to stay."

Father and son stood nose to nose glaring at each other, and for one heart-stopping moment, Gina thought they would exchange blows, and the way her brothers moved towards the two men, they obviously thought so too, but Darius swung on his heel and strode away before the situation could escalate out of control. Shortly after, they heard the front door slam with some force. Gina ran to the window in time to see her brother striding angrily over to his car carrying a small case. Then he climbed into the vehicle, and with an angry spurt of gravel, he had driven off.

After two days with no sign of Darius, the family began to worry. "Where the devil is he?" his father thundered. "He could at least have the decency to let us know that he's all right."

The anxiety in her father's voice made Gina angry at her brother's inexcusable behaviour. It was unusual for Darius to conduct himself like this. He was always so thoughtful as a rule, so meticulous in keeping appointments and informing the family if a sudden business deal necessitated him leaving the country at a moment's notice. Now to just go off without a word was not on. Gina knew, even if her brother did not, that he was acting totally out of character with this girl. He was in love; she was sure of it. She also knew that Darius had always steered clear and would fight against any sort of entanglement that would commit him permanently to anyone, but this was one girl that he could not just use and walk away from, no matter how much he tried to pass it off as a fleeting attraction. Deep down inside, Darius knew that, and so he fought against the feelings that were consuming him. Gina laughed to herself; he was certainly failing in that respect. She made up her mind to visit Jenny.

ꀈ ꀈ ꀈ ꀈ ꀈ ꀈ

Jenny stood staring miserably out of the shop at the rain slanting down outside the window. It certainly kept the customers at bay. Her gaze was caught by the unexpected sight of Isabel across the street, huddling under an umbrella. This was strange to say the least, and she felt a flicker of alarm. Now what on earth was someone like Isabel doing in a quiet out of the way place like this? It was a long way to come just to do a little shopping. A dark-haired, extremely attractive woman accompanied Isabel. One who Jenny had last seen at the party, and she was turning to speak to the man inside the car next to her. Jenny felt her heart jump as she saw it was Darius, then she felt an explosion of pain as the woman leaned down and planted a firm kiss on his mouth. Jenny turned away, her pulse beating hard with hurt and anger. So that must be the mysterious Melissa, the woman who had captured his heart.

"I'll bet she doesn't know that he's got wandering hands, the slimy snake. How dare he!" Jenny fumed. Vengeful thoughts vied with the heartache that she was experiencing. As if to add to her misery, she was horrified to see that Isabel, with her companion in tow, was making a determined beeline towards her shop. Fortunately, there was no sign of Darius, who seemed to have disappeared, having him walk in with them would have been just too much to bear.

The shop bell tinkled, and Jenny pretended to concentrate on sorting out a box of toys behind the counter, before glancing up with a polite smile. "Can I be of some assistance?" she inquired, looking straight through Isabel, as though she had never seen her before.

Isabel tightened her lips, then showed her teeth in the travesty of a smile. "I cannot believe that your memory is that appallingly bad, my dear. By the way, this is Melissa. I expect Gina will have told you all about her." Her eyes were glittering and hard as she ushered the girl forward. She indicated Jenny, saying to Melissa. "This is one of James's little friends."

The young woman moved her lips slightly in the semblance of a smile and then drifted off to inspect one of the shelves stacked with books.

"Pretty girl, isn't she?" drawled Isabel maliciously. "So suited to Darius, don't you think? Both families are absolutely thrilled at the news. Your sister and yourself, as friends of James, are, of course, invited to the engagement party."

Jenny fought hard not to let her feelings show, but her white face gave her away as she gazed back at this hideous woman. "Congratulations! Is there anything you would like to buy?" Jenny indicated the gifts on the counter, trying to keep her voice even.

"I really don't think there is anything here that would suit me, do you?" Isabel gave a tinkling laugh that made Jenny want to pull all her teeth out. One by one. Slowly. Jenny's eyes fell on the old besom broom, and she was sorely tempted to point it out to Isabel, but her inherent politeness made her restrain herself.

Melissa had her back to them as she glanced idly along the books and overheard Isabel's words, despite the lowered hissing tone. She smiled triumphantly. It suited her own ambitions for Isabel to see her as a potential wife for Darius. She was thrilled at this boost to her own campaign. It irritated her to know that despite her best efforts to be there when he needed her, as a companion to attend parties, or to invite her to make numbers up for dinner, Darius did not appear to be remotely interested in her as a romantic partner. He saw her purely as a family friend.

"Well, we must be off," Isabel trilled. "I just called in to give you the good news. Now we simply must run. Darius insisted on giving us a lift and he really does not like to be kept waiting." What she did not mention was that Darius was sitting in his car fuming at the fact that he had been coerced by his father into giving the two women a lift. There was no way in the state that he was in over Jenny that he would have come here of his own volition. Darius had also noted the possessive kiss that Melissa had given him, taking him by surprise, he just hoped that Jenny had not witnessed it too. Why, he was not sure, because it didn't really matter anymore.

𒑲 𒑲 𒑲 𒑲 𒑲

Isabel swept triumphantly out of the shop, ushering Melissa before her and slammed the door loudly, leaving Jenny feeling utterly and completely shattered. When Rachel came into the shop shortly after, she found her sister staring off into space with suspiciously red eyes.

"What did that evil woman want and what did she say to upset you? I saw her gloating face as she walked away. Have you been crying?" she asked, rattling the questions off at Jenny.

"Nothing that I didn't know already, and no, I have not been crying." Jenny shook her head. "I think I'm catching a cold. In fact, I don't think I will do any more designing today. Perhaps a dose of fresh air will make me feel better."

"You do look a bit washed out." Rachel nodded, peering more closely at her. "Why don't you go and have some coffee before you go out, and do remember to take your umbrella." She watched as Jenny closed the shop door behind her, not for one moment fooled by such a flimsy excuse. They both became blotchy when crying. That gruesome woman, and for that matter, Darius, had an awful lot to answer for.

𒑲 𒑲 𒑲 𒑲 𒑲

Gina tapped on the shop door the next morning. She knew it was Rachel's day off, and that she was out with James so Jenny should be alone. There was no answer and yet she could see Jenny's hunched figure seated at a table, silhouetted by the sunlight slanting through the back of the shop. She tapped again and Jenny came reluctantly to open the door.

"Hello, Gina," she said dully. "What can I do for you?"

"Well, for a start you could let me in!"

"Oh, sorry, Gina. Do come in, although I am not sure that we have anything to talk about," Jenny said with a mournful sigh.

"Honestly, you two, you make a fine pair!" Gina put her hands on her hips, with an exasperated look on her face.

"Pardon?"

"Darius and you! He has been an absolute pain in the butt, and you look as though you have spent all your time moping about. What is wrong with you both? He has just turned up after three days' absence, no explanation and in no better mood, I can assure you. Why can't you just go out together, scratch your itch, and get each other out of your systems?"

As Gina spoke, she saw the wounded look in Jenny's eyes and was secretly pleased at this evidence of Jenny's true feelings. "I'm sorry, that was crass of me. It obviously means more to you than just a quick fling."

"You mean unlike Darius. He could deal with it easily that way, I suppose. Then he could just walk away." Jenny smiled sadly.

Gina could tell by the shuttered look on Jenny's face that any plea on her brother's behalf would fall on stony ground, so she changed tactics. "Look, Darius has business dealings over in France during the coming week, starting this Friday. Why don't you come and stay with us for the weekend, just for one night if you are worried that he might come back early." She saw the look of doubt on Jenny's face and adopted a wheedling tone. "Isabel and father are in Portugal at the moment, so you see, it will only be us and the boys, and Rachel, of course. If I know James, he will already have asked her now the cat's away."

"I don't know. I have a lot of work on."

"Oh, come on, what do you say? The weather forecast is for sun and yet more sun. It will be marvellous, and we can picnic down by the boat." Gina watched the indecision in her expression, as Jenny stared back, her imagination caught.

"Boat?"

"Oh, it's only a small cabin cruiser," Gina laughed. "We keep it moored on the river down beyond the bottom pasture. It's truly beautiful there, you will love it."

Jenny was very tempted, despite her reservations about setting foot anywhere near his house again. The fact that Isabel and Darius were going to be absent finally persuaded her. She made up her mind, it would be a welcome diversion.

ℸ ℸ ℸ ℸ ℸ ℸ

Jenny pushed her misgivings to the back of her mind as she packed a small bag and set off determined to enjoy the weekend. Gina showed her over the small boat and Jenny loved it, although the other girl's idea of being small was pretty inaccurate. Jenny had pictured something tiny, with a box-like cabin for two. Six people could sleep comfortably here, and there was a large sun deck on top which drew her like a magnet. Jenny could just imagine stretching out comfortably on that warm surface. Yes, she would certainly enjoy herself here.

"Now, remember," Gina said. "Make yourself at home and enjoy the peace while you can. The picnic will be tomorrow, so for today just relax and listen to the sound of the river talking." She rummaged through one of the tiny lockers and triumphantly held up a minuscule bikini. "I knew I had a spare on board. Here, try it on."

"Gina! I cannot possibly wear that piece of string. I might as well be naked." Jenny raised her eyebrows in horror at the thought of displaying that much flesh.

"Don't be so stuffy, Jenny. Who on earth is going to see you down here anyway? The boys are off to a rugby match, and I am off to Aunt Edna's for a while, so relax. Go and have a nice laze in all that lovely sunshine." Gina giggled, as she threw the offending garment at Jenny. "I won't be long, maybe an hour or so, then I will join you and soak up some of that sunshine for myself."

"Thank you, I think," Jenny said, as she gingerly held the tiny pieces of string up between her fingers.

"Remember, make the most of that sunshine." Gina grabbed her bag, ran up the steps onto the small plank that served as a gangway and jumped onto the bank. Then she was off, trotting along the track back up to the house.

Jenny lay totally relaxed, basking in the warmth of the sun, feeling the soft summer breeze playing over her bare skin, and sighed with pure bliss. This definitely beats sitting huddled over my drawing board, she thought lazily. At first, Jenny had been reluctant to don the tiny bikini, but the lure of the sun had gradually lowered her inhibitions, and she had given in. Now she was grateful she had. She lost track of time as she drifted off into a light doze, and when she felt the boat rock, she assumed that it was Gina, having come back sooner than intended. A shadow falling over her made Jenny open her eyes, her words of greeting drying in her throat as she looked up.

Darius stood over her, his muscular legs on either side of hers, looking down at her near-naked figure. He only wore brief shorts, and they did nothing to disguise his desire. The strength and size of his body was overwhelming. He was a solidly built man, perfectly proportioned. A deep tan covered the glistening skin stretched over the powerful shoulders and long limbs, adding to his attraction. Her eyes gazed at the dark hair on his chest, which only added to his strong masculine presence, and she swallowed nervously as she felt her own helpless response to this giant of a man.

Jenny stared at Darius, transfixed, and even had she wanted to, was incapable of movement. She felt boneless and naked under his smouldering gaze and had still made no effort to avoid him, as he dropped to his knees and straddled her quivering body. As Jenny felt him lowering himself down onto her, she came to life and lifted her arms to stop him.

"No," Darius said huskily. "Don't fight me." Then he grabbed her hands and held them above her head, letting his full weight descend on her.

"You mustn't," Jenny gave a small gasping moan, as she felt his hard body make contact. She jumped as he took her wrists in one hand and ran the other down to her breast. With one sharp snap of material, her top was disposed of. A feeling of panic invaded her as his hand travelled downwards, and began to explore and caress her, disposing with the other flimsy remnant of material just as easily.

Darius let go of her hands and his mouth took hers with such passion that Jenny felt as though she was melting. Her treacherous arms slid around his powerful body, and she felt him tremble as her hands caressed him. The resultant movements of his body only served to fuel her own desire. Suddenly he was lifting her hips, pushing against her and she went rigid.

"We mustn't, this is madness," Jenny moaned, making a feeble attempt at resistance.

Darius looked down at her through narrowed glittering eyes. His face was flushed as he whispered hoarsely. "I have to, we have to. You are driving me mad, you witch. I have to exorcise you." Then with one hard thrust, he took her, and as her body arched instinctively towards him, the movement pushed Darius over the edge and he lost control, taking her with him on that timeless journey. As the passion exploded between them, Jenny's mind shattered into a thousand sparkling pieces and spiralled away. She was helplessly lost, only aware of the touch of his hard body against her own, and finally drifted back to reality as she felt his last convulsive shudder.

Darius rolled sideways, drawing in air to fill his lungs, trying to gain control of his breathing and body, one arm still holding Jenny firmly against him. "God, I am sorry. Are you all right? I don't normally act like such an animal." He lifted his head, gazing down into her flushed, dazed face and said softly. "Speak to me."

"I don't know what to say," Jenny said shakily, as she looked up at him and saw the way his eyes were lingering on her soft exposed breasts. Her own desire was once more clamouring for release and she groaned as Darius pressed her hand against his body, making her very aware that he wanted her again. Jenny knew that this must not happen and had to fight hard to curb her own base impulses. He must think that from the way she had mindlessly given in that she was easy. This time, Jenny pulled away so quickly that she took him by surprise. Before Darius could stop her, she had scrambled to her feet, grabbed the towel she had been lying on and draped it around herself protectively. Jenny backed away, as he climbed to his feet.

"No! And I mean no, this time. This should never have happened. I never do this sort of thing; I don't indulge in casual sex." She blushed hotly at his raised brows and stammered. "I don't know what came over me."

"What harm did it do? Why not just enjoy the moment? I want you and you seem to want me." Darius stared longingly at her, and his voice became almost pleading as he edged nearer.

"There's no future in it. We differ so much in our outlook." Jenny gave a shaky sigh, moving back from his advancing body. "We're better off not meeting again."

She was grateful that, by now, Darius had slipped his shorts back on. He was overwhelming enough with clothes on, without them he was magnificent and distracting.

"Nobody says that there has to be a future. Can't we just enjoy what we have while it lasts?" He looked down at her with a growing frown of frustration.

Jenny's head jerked up and she studied his face. It was devoid of expression, and he was holding himself rigid. "That is so cold-blooded. I can't have a relationship purely based on lust," she said, as a feeling of humiliation washed over her. Darius obviously thought he could just use her and then when he was finally bored, dispose of her. Jenny turned her back on him and marched away, climbing down into the cabin. She dressed swiftly and furiously, hating him and herself. Yet she could hardly blame him. She had not exactly offered much resistance to his advances, which had provoked his heated response. It had certainly not been one-sided, so it was no wonder that he felt frustrated.

Darius stood where she had left him, his hands hanging at his sides, feeling helpless. He had never experienced this loss of power before. He was usually an extremely contained and articulate man. Yet where Jenny was concerned, his brain seemed to cease to function normally, and all the wrong words poured from his mouth. She would now think of him as a predatory male, who simply saw her as an easy target. On the other hand, he mused, she had allowed it to happen. He felt desire rise as he remembered the feel of her body under his. A look of determination spread over his face, and he made his way purposefully down to the cabin. He hesitated in the doorway, as he realised that Jenny was hastily packing her small bag.

"Where are you going?" he demanded, moving forward as though to stop her.

"Away from this place, away from you," Jenny said, holding the bag up defensively in front of her body.

"Why?" His face was set and white.

"Darius, after what just occurred, I think that's obvious, don't you?" She frowned at him. Jenny tried to school her features into an uncaring expression. She desperately wanted to leave before her composure cracked. She wanted to be able to scream and cry at the unfairness of life, in letting her fall in love with a man who was incapable of returning that love, and that she was desperately in love with him was beyond dispute. Jenny had never given herself to any man with that much abandon before. Not that there had been many. She shivered with embarrassment as she pushed past his unmoving body and made her escape.

ꙡ ꙡ ꙡ ꙡ ꙡ ꙡ

When Gina arrived back at the boat looking forward to a relaxing hour or so, she was surprised to find no sign of Jenny, and her brother sitting on the bunk, his head in his hands.

"Where is Jenny?" she asked.

"Gone." His voice was muffled as Darius spoke. "And won't be coming back, as long as I'm here."

She looked down at his dark head and her heart swelled with compassion for her brother. Gina shook her head despairingly as she asked softly, "What have you said to upset her now?"

"It's not what I've said, it's what I've done," Darius answered, as he dropped his hands and lifted his head.

"Oh! Darius, you are a fool at times." His sister was shocked at the desolation she saw in his eyes and guessed what had occurred between the two. "It's really not what happened, but how you handled it afterwards. The damage is not irreparable, is it? Can't you go to her and explain how you feel?"

"What should I say? 'I want you, would you consent to be my mistress until you get fed up with me?'" Darius laughed harshly. He stood up slowly, pulling himself together. "She's probably got plenty of men dangling on a string, why would she settle for me?"

"Have you let her know that you love her?" Gina smiled understandingly.

"Love! Don't be so bloody stupid, Gina." He flushed angrily. "I'm just a victim of my hormones at the moment. It will pass. Anyway, she doesn't love me."

"I see, so all this misery is caused by your hormones, is it?" His sister folded her arms and glared at him. She would ignore the title of stupid. Sometimes Gina felt as though she could slap Darius.

"I have no wish to discuss this subject further. Let's drop it, shall we?" Darius brushed past her and clambered up the steps to the deck. Then he was gone, making his way hastily down onto the small mooring jetty.

Gina stood on the boat, watching her brother's progress up the track to the field beyond, with troubled eyes. "My, my, he has got it bad," she murmured to herself. Something had to be done!

When Jenny reached the house, she found to her distress that Rachel had arranged to stay for yet another party. "I can't stay here any longer, Rachel, and you don't need me to hold your hand."

Rachel looked more closely at her as she heard the tremor in her sister's voice and noticed the agitated way she was rubbing her folded arms. "What's wrong, Jenny, why are you so upset?"

"I can't talk about it, not now." Her sister shook her head. "I'm sorry, but I have to leave."

"You can't leave before the party, Jenny." A voice from the open doorway made them both jump. It was James, and he added blithely, completely unaware of her distress, "I won't hear of it. We organised it especially for you two girls. It will be fun." He left, promising to come and escort them down later when they were ready.

Jenny sank weakly down onto her bed. Why do people insist on involving me in things that I really do not want to do, she thought wearily. Jenny shivered as she felt the tender bruised feeling in her body, evidence of her own stupidity, and felt like weeping.

"I've got nothing to wear, so that lets me off the hook." She turned with a faint smile of relief to Rachel. "You go down and enjoy yourself, I'm going to pack."

Jenny slid off the bed and picked up her bag, throwing it onto the chair and unzipping it. Then she grabbed the little she had brought with her for the day, and bundled everything haphazardly inside the bag, then zipped it firmly shut.

"You can borrow something of mine," Gina said from the doorway.

"What is this, Piccadilly Circus," muttered Jenny crossly. "The last time I borrowed something of yours, it led to embarrassing complications."

"I know." Gina gave her a wicked smile.

Jenny blushed furiously, and her sister looked at her with curiosity. What was she not being told?

"By the way, I thought it might interest you to know that Darius has finally left for France. You are free and clear of potential problems," Gina added, as she made to leave the room. She gave Jenny a conspiratorial smile as she left. "I will bring the dress to you in just a moment."

Rachel gave her sister a narrow-eyed look. "What's going on?"

"Nothing of any importance is going on, as you put it!" Jenny said, in a dismissive tone. "Just feeling a little jaded, that's all."

"What you need is a pick me up," her sister said, with a consoling pat on the arm. "There will be nibbles and wine, so that should do the trick."

Gina returned with the promised dress, and Jenny eyed it warily as she held it up. Good job that Daruis would not be attending, because that neckline looked a bit too low for her. She supposed it hardly mattered now. After tonight there was no way she would ever enter this house again.

Chapter Nine

Jenny stood unhappily, watching the party unfolding around her, feeling totally detached from it all. To add to her depression was the fact that Isabel and Charles had returned earlier than expected from their holiday. Jenny put her hand to her throat and gave a faint smile as her fingers encountered one of the beautifully jewelled necklaces that Gina had insisted on both girls wearing. They had tried to refuse as the jewels were obviously valuable, but Gina was adamant. "Please," she said, "Just for tonight." They had been her mother's, and Charles had raised no objection. She was wearing one herself and besides, their dresses needed something a little more glamorous to jazz them up, so they had gracefully accepted. The dress Gina had chosen for Jenny looked better than she had anticipated, and she felt more confident about her appearance. Now here she was, all dolled up and not enjoying herself one bit.

Isabel's eyes had instantly homed in on the jewels, and at the sight of the necklace around Jenny's neck, she had felt utterly enraged. She had not yet seen that Rachel was also similarly adorned. Those jewels had belonged to Charles's first wife, and he had never offered them for her to wear. It was an affront to her pride, and jealousy burned within her, growing out of proportion. Why was that dreadful girl wearing it? Had she been making a play for Charles? Her eyes narrowed, or one of the other boys? Isabel had thought that she had put paid to any ambitions the girl had as far as Darius was concerned, but what of Darius himself? She had noticed his preoccupation of late. Had Jenny somehow persuaded him to part with the necklace? Isabel could no longer contain herself and she made a determined beeline for Jenny.

The first moment Jenny was aware of her presence was when a sharp-nailed hand grabbed her arm viciously. "Did Darius give you that?" Isabel hissed, her eyes fixed accusingly on the jewels around Jenny's neck.

"No, he did not!" Jenny retorted, indignantly, snatching her arm away.

"I thought not. He would never give them to a little tramp like you." Then Isabel added nastily. "Darius does not have to buy his favours, my dear."

Jenny whitened, gasping with anger and took an involuntary step back. Isabel gave a satisfied smile at the stricken look on Jenny's face. "You are quite right, he did not give it to me," Jenny said quietly, as she calmed herself. "It was kindly lent by Gina to enhance my dress, but I should hate to cause family friction. Here, take it!" Jenny reached up, undid the necklace and held it out, wishing that she could stuff it down that elegant throat. By now people had become aware of the tension between the two and were gravitating towards them.

As Isabel went to take the necklace, Jenny moved her hand aside and gave the jewels to Charles, who was standing behind and to one side of his wife. He stared down at the necklace in his hand silently, then turned and studied his wife's flushed face.

"I should not like it to go astray and be accused of stealing it." Jenny looked pointedly at Isabel and added. "Now I suppose I had better take my leave, before you ask me to go."

Jenny glanced around at the mixture of disapproving expressions on the guest's faces. She did not much care if the looks were directed at her or Isabel, and Jenny gave a slight derisive smile, saying with quiet dignity as she walked from the room, "Enjoy your party."

Rachel followed closely behind her, just stopping long enough to drop her necklace into Charles still open palm as she left. "Here, you will want this one, as well."

"How dare she speak to you like that, Jen. I could strangle her, the bitch," Rachel raged, furious and upset.

"Now can we *please* go home?" Jenny said quietly, feeling drained of emotion.

Rachel rushed to her side and put her arms around her. She hated to see Jenny like this. Her sister was normally so cheerful, and nothing seemed to get her down as a rule. It frightened Rachel to see this change. Something told her that it was more than just that unfortunate business downstairs.

Jenny would have laughed if she had felt up to it, because it was strange to see her usually placid sister so up in arms, ready to take on the appalling Isabel for her.

James came rushing up into their room and was as angry about the whole affair as Rachel. He begged them not to leave until Isabel had been made to apologise.

"No, James, apologies will not change how your mother feels about us," Jenny said, sadly.

Rachel reached up and kissed his worried face, as he asked anxiously if this would make any difference to how she felt about him. "No! You big oaf, I can't just stop loving you because of someone else's unpleasantness. I know Isabel is your mother, and this makes it difficult for you, so it's better if we leave until you have had time to talk with her." She squeezed his waist reassuringly, and James slowly relaxed as he watched them gather their belongings together. James drove them home and did not need much persuading to stay the night. He did not care to face his mother for a while, because there would certainly be quite a confrontation when he did return home, and besides, it was a long journey back.

"On the sofa," Rachel said softly, as he made to follow her into her bedroom. He groaned and she giggled, nodding meaningfully at Jenny's closed door. She had to find out what was making her sister so unhappy, apart from that nasty scene at the party.

꙰꙰꙰꙰꙰꙰

Rachel managed, over the next few days, to glean from little pieces of information that Jenny let slip, roughly what had occurred. She did not see it as the problem that her sister did. Why couldn't Jenny just enjoy herself with Darius? She was obviously quite attracted to him and why did she think that nothing could come of it?

"You don't understand, Rachel," her sister said. "Darius is not like James. He uses women and discards them, even Gina had to admit that, and I am not going to join his cast-offs. Besides, I heard Isabel saying that his wedding to Melissa is imminent. As far as he's concerned, any feelings he has for me are just pure lust."

"Oh, I am so sorry, sis. I didn't realise that Darius was already contemplating marriage with Melissa. That puts a whole different perspective on his behaviour. What a rotten way to treat you and her. Poor girl. How dare he!"

"Well, at least I won't have to see him again, so I can put it all behind me and get on with my life," Jenny murmured, unable to hide the desolation in her eyes.

"You more than liked him, didn't you?" Rachel probed. She watched her sister anxiously, hoping her feelings for Darius were not too deep.

"What does it matter now?" Jenny shrugged. "It's over, so best forgotten."

Rachel decided to drop the subject. All it did was cloud the air, and her sister was right. It was best not to discuss it further, because it would achieve nothing.

꙰꙰꙰꙰꙰꙰

Darius immersed himself in work, trying to occupy his mind, but his distraction was obvious to his fellow associates.

"Are you all right, Darius?" one of them queried. They were trying to sort a business problem out, and his uncharacteristic silence was a cause for concern.

"Pardon? Why should there be anything wrong?" he snapped. Darius turned and stared stonily at the man, then sighed, as he saw the annoyed expression on his colleague's face. "Sorry, Peter." He rubbed his forehead. "I guess I'm just tired. Perhaps I'm sickening for something. I think I'll leave early and make a long weekend of it."

His friend patted him on the shoulder in commiseration. "Good idea, Darius, you never take enough time off. Go and enjoy your weekend."

Darius could not get Jenny out of his mind. His unhappiness was eating at him, eroding his concentration, driving him mad. His desire was an all-consuming, constant companion. He had, of course, taken his share of women, yet had never felt like this before. That it could be love was something he shied away from. Darius just knew that this was unfinished business, and he had to see her again.

Chapter Ten

The weeks drifted by and Jenny buried herself in her work, or tried to. More often than not, she found herself staring into space and thinking about Darius. He had tried to talk to her on the telephone, had called once in person, but she would not see him. Even James had been enlisted to try and reason with her, but Jenny would have none of it. She loved Darius too much just to be used to assuage his passion. She could not handle the hurt she knew it would cause when his obsession had run its course, and what about Melissa?

Jenny dwelt enviously on the happiness between her sister and James. He truly seemed to be deeply in love with Rachel, showing it in various small ways and trying to spend all his spare moments with her. Rachel, in turn, was always talking about him, her face softening as she spoke of James, hesitating occasionally as though she were afraid of upsetting Jenny with her constant talk of her love for him.

Jenny sighed, something that she had been doing a great deal of lately, and decided to go and eat. At least she had food as a comfort, although lately Jenny had not eaten much. She sighed dismally once again. James had taken Rachel away for a romantic weekend, and Jenny was by herself in the flat when the doorbell rang. She was taken by surprise, when as soon as she opened the door, Darius pushed past her.

"We have to talk," he said, in a clipped voice.

"No, we don't," she mumbled, taken aback. Jenny held her hands clasped tightly against her chest, doing her best to still her fast-beating heart and trying not to reach out to him. She wanted so much to touch him, but that mustn't happen. Where is your backbone? she asked herself. Get a grip!

"We need to," he insisted.

"We have nothing to say, Darius. You're wasting your time." She stared at his white, strained face and found herself worrying about him. He looked almost ill.

"Please, Jenny, just listen to me. We have something. I'm not sure what yet and I know that you feel it too. All I know is that you're driving me mad, and I have to be able to see you, touch you, hold you." As Darius spoke, despite his resolution to just talk, his hands reached out and grasped her shoulders firmly, drawing her suddenly pliant body close to his, and he rasped hoarsely. "I need you."

Jenny could feel his hot breath fanning her lips as his head slowly lowered, his mouth blindly seeking hers. She tried to push away, but his superior strength made her efforts useless. To make matters worse, her own treacherous body was aiding and abetting him, weakly melting against him, encouraging his pulsating arousal. She felt his heart pounding against her, and the way that he trembled as he moved closer to her.

Darius lost whatever control he had left and without taking his mouth from hers, he picked her up and moved purposefully towards her bedroom. Her good intentions were further eroded, as he lay her on the bed following her body down with his, searching hands running over her feverishly in his haste to divest her of her clothing.

His mouth and tongue seemed to be drawing the soul from her body, and Jenny felt as though she were fusing with him. Her heart was beating in time to the movements of his restless seeking loins, and she felt as though the heat between them would ultimately consume her. A sudden fear coursed through her, as she felt him pushing insistently against her, waking a spark of sanity as Jenny realised that, once again, she was allowing all this to happen, and she stiffened with resistance.

Darius felt her sudden withdrawal and his hands began a slow, seductive exploration of her body. His lips released her mouth and slid down to the fullness of her breasts, touching them with his tongue, drawing on the moist peaks, making her whimper with pleasure and driving all coherent thought from her head. Jenny felt his hands moving her legs gently apart, probing fingers touching her intimately, until an explosion of feeling rendered her totally mindless, her legs opening helplessly to accommodate his first tentative thrust.

As her body responded to his, Darius shuddered, no longer able to contain himself and slid into her. At the feel of her soft inner warmth, he lost his head completely, thrusting almost savagely into her, beginning that age-old pounding rhythm, sending their minds soaring to unimaginable heights. Ultimately it had to end, and they crashed to earth together, their hearts beating erratically.

Darius drew a shuddering breath as he collapsed on top of her. He looked down into her flushed face, Jenny's eyes were still closed, and he felt fiercely protective as he held her shaking body, stroking her with gentle hands. Darius wanted to bind her so close that she became part of him, to completely possess her, as she had him.

Jenny felt his arms tighten as his desire throbbed against her, and she drew her breath in as his mouth sought hers and he took her again. Darius seemed to be insatiable, not withdrawing from her, holding her firmly against his body. Half sleeping, waking to begin again, until tiredness finally overcame even his awesome stamina.

Jenny just lay quietly, looking at him. Darius slept, his arms still around her, almost as though he was frightened to let go, in case she disappeared. In sleep, Darius looked vulnerable, and tears filled her eyes as her heart swelled with love for him. Did he feel as she did when they made love, or was it just sexual gratification that he felt? Jenny was too tired to dwell on the problem and snuggled up to him, making the most of his closeness while she could, before finally joining him in oblivion.

நநநநநந

The call came just as the early morning sun was filtering through a gap in the curtains. Darius cursed and groped around with one hand to locate his mobile, talking quietly, not wanting to disturb Jenny. His face softened, as he gazed down at her. The wild tangle of silken curls was spread out over the pillow, and her soft pink lips were slightly parted as she breathed. Jenny slept soundly as though she was exhausted, and a reminiscent smile curved his lips as Darius recalled the events that had led to her somnolent state. It was so tempting to take advantage of the moment, but he had to leave, so he reluctantly slid from the bed.

He dressed quickly, leaning over and touching Jenny's lips tenderly with his own, not wanting to leave her. A strange fear possessed him. It had been good, too good. He loved her so much, he finally admitted that fact to himself now, and was afraid that something would happen to spoil it. He shut the bedroom door quietly and walked to the front door. As Darius went to open it, he hesitated and turned back. He wrote a brief note and left it on a side table, propped up by a small flower he had taken from the vase that stood nearby.

The call that Darius had received was important and could not be ignored. His presence was required to settle a dispute that had developed over one small sentence in a contract. Stupid on the surface, and yet a lot of people were awaiting the outcome, so he would have to negotiate between the two warring sides. Sometimes Darius lost patience with people's stupidity and yet he also was well aware that the wording in a contract could make a great deal of difference to any disputes in the future. So he had to leave Jenny, when all Darius wanted to do was bury himself in her forever. He could almost be tempted to climb back into that warm and welcoming bed, and had she been awake, he may just have done that and to hell with the consequences.

Darius walked up the gravel path and made for his car. In his haste to get underway, he failed to spot Melissa, who had been for an early morning horse ride and was standing talking to one of the women from the school where she stabled her horse.

ཀྐཀྐཀྐ

Melissa glanced up and her words froze on her lips as she saw where Darius had emerged from, and a black rage filled her. The woman she was speaking to was taken aback by the venom in Melissa's expression and bid her a hasty farewell. Melissa hardly glanced at her as she made her escape, she was too busy fuming. Now what was he doing calling on that shop girl at this early hour? There was only one reason to her mind for Darius to have been here. A little affair on the side she could turn a blind eye to. Unless... She felt a frisson of alarm, was he seriously attracted to this girl? Darius was her meal ticket and Melissa had made too many plans based on a future as his wife, not that he was aware of that yet. She was not about to see him stolen from under her nose by some little nobody. Her anger drove her to take instant action.

Melissa marched across the road and up the gravel path, then was surprised when the small door at the side of the cottage opened easily. She made her way up to the flat and knocked loudly, then nearly fell in as that too swung open. Good grief hadn't the stupid girl ever heard of security? The first thing Melissa noticed as she entered was the note written in Darius's firm hand and propped up on the table. She snatched it up and read it with increasing rage, then screwed it up and thrust the offending message into her pocket. So, that little gold digger was waiting for Darius to return and sort their future out, was she? Well, she would have something to say about that! Melissa thought carefully about her next move and smiled maliciously, as she approached the bedroom door. She knocked on the door angrily with the side of her fist.

Jenny was startled by the imperious knocking at the door and sat up dazedly, blinking her eyes at the unexpected noise. She groaned as she felt the stiffness in her limbs, and the bruised sensation in her body. Jenny smiled softly, dreamily, then jumped as the knocking began again, only now registering that someone was in the flat, and that Darius had gone. She wrapped a sheet tightly around herself and staggered to the door. As she opened it, Melissa brushed by her and stood with her hands on her hips, glaring malevolently at her.

"You little tramp. It's bad enough that I have to keep paying his latest flings off, but you! You are too close to home. How dare you use your friendship with James to get close to Darius. This small interlude won't make any difference, you know. The marriage is still on."

Jenny stared at her, feeling as though she had woken up in the middle of a nightmare. "How did you know that Darius had been here?" she asked inanely, her senses having temporarily deserted her.

"How do you think I knew? Here! That should pay for it, I think." Jenny was shocked when the angry woman facing her threw a wad of money onto the bed. "It's a little more than he usually pays. Probably because you are Rachel's sister, which makes you a bit more difficult to dispose of. James will be highly embarrassed by all this."

Jenny shook herself out of her trance-like state and found her voice, then gave a disbelieving laugh,. "Oh, for goodness sake, stop being so theatrical, Melissa. You sound like something out of a Victorian melodrama. Apart from anything else, Darius would never have to pay a woman for her favours."

Melissa stared at her and then turned abruptly away, her eyes narrowing, thinking hard. This girl was not as stupid as she appeared. She felt like screaming with rage at the fact that Jenny had managed to attain the position in his affections she herself aspired to, and Melissa could not bear it. When she turned back, her eyes were swimming with tears, and she was biting her lip pathetically.

"I am so sorry, and of course, you are quite right. I have no pride as far as Darius is concerned, I'm afraid. I love him so much. What is true are his constant affairs. I am always left with the unpleasant task of clearing the damage up. He has gone off to France to escape, as he usually does, I might add. Even I am losing patience with his endless pursuit of women. That will all change when we're married, of course."

"I don't believe all this. Darius would not do this to me," Jenny stated firmly.

Melissa blinked her tears away and delicately dabbed at her eyes. "I can see why you need to convince yourself, and I suppose you think that you are in love with him. Well, I am sorry, because nothing will ever come of it. Darius told me you might be a bit clingy."

A niggle of uncertainty was taking hold of Jenny's mind, and she sank down slowly onto the bed, frowning curiously up at the other woman. "Why do you stay with him, if he is as bad as you make out?"

"Because he is a good catch, as you no doubt have found out, and I can put up with a few non-threatening affairs from time to time, but it does become a little wearing after a while." Melissa folded her arms and looked down at her pityingly. "Now as the wedding draws nearer, I think it's time to curtail his little antics, wouldn't you agree?"

"Oh, yes, the wedding," Jenny said, feeling as though she were dying inside.

"Don't tell me that you've conveniently forgotten his previous commitments in your haste to bed him?" Melissa raised her brows, forgetting to maintain her hurt look, as nastiness got the better of her. "I should think that being told he was engaged would have been enough of a hint. Are you incredibly stupid as well as promiscuous?"

"Get out," Jenny cried, incensed, and jumped up taking a threatening step forward.

"I would have thought that it was patently obvious that I am the wronged party here," Melissa said, backing away at the fury on Jenny's face.

"Yes, I guess you are," Jenny said, quietly, as she subsided. She was at fault, Jenny knew that, and she felt incredibly guilty. How could she have forgotten his engagement? She had been carried away by the moment, but what of Darius? Was it just convenient to forget his promise to Melissa, and was there some truth in her allegations about his many conquests? "There will be no further meetings, I assure you."

Jenny raised her wounded eyes to Melissa's and said in a low voice, "Now, if you don't mind, I want to be alone."

"You know it has to end, so I will leave you to come to terms with your conscience, and trust you will do the right thing," the other girl stated, with a contemptuous twist of the lips.

Jenny made no reply. What could she say? She had no defence against Melissa's accusations if they were true! When the door closed behind her unwelcome visitor, she collapsed tiredly back upon the bed. Shock had rendered her immobile and she felt numb. She lay staring blankly at the ceiling, going over their conversation. The things that Melissa had said were ludicrous and yet... Jenny turned and gazed at the imprint of Darius's head on the pillow. He had left without waking her or making plans to meet again.

She had, once again, in a moment of weakness, given in to her love for him and she had been so firm in her decision not to let him use her, yet one touch had scattered her resolutions to the winds. Had Darius just been using her, getting her out of his system? No, she could not believe that of him. A small nagging voice in her head reminded her that he had made no promises, no words of love had passed his lips. In fact, they had hardly talked at all. Jenny blushed as she thought of what had taken up most of their time. She groaned to herself, at her own reckless and wanton behaviour.

"I wish I could cry," she whispered, forlornly. Jenny finally dragged herself to her feet with a feeling of impending dread, and decided to wait to hear from Darius, and see what he had to say.

Chapter Eleven

No matter how much Jenny looked at the phone, it did not ring. The day dragged on interminably and when by late evening the phone still remained silent, she sank dejectedly into the small armchair, feeling a deep despair. When it finally rang, shock coursed through her body, making her shake. She picked it up with trembling hands and answered quietly, holding her breath, waiting with trepidation for the caller to speak. The sound of Gina's voice made her heart sink.

"Hello, Jenny, I just wondered if you would like to go on a shopping spree with me tomorrow. I thought with Rachel away, you might like some company. Hello? Are you there?"

"Gina, where is Darius?" Jenny asked in a thready whisper, as she gripped the phone tightly. There was no instant reply, and Jenny felt her hopes crash entirely.

"He's in France. Why do you ask?" Gina answered slowly, questioningly.

Jenny stared at the phone and wanted to throw it down, then swallowed her pride. "Did Darius leave a message for me? Has he mentioned me at all?" The silence was a little longer this time.

"Well, no, but then he left very early, so probably didn't have time to tell anyone he was going, but Darius is bound to call later to let father know his whereabouts. Shall I tell him you rang, is there any message?"

"No, and please don't say that I phoned. It was only something trivial, nothing important." Jenny angrily dashed the stinging tears from her eyes, then she put the phone down, sinking back down into her chair and giving in to her misery.

Gina replaced the receiver, her face thoughtful. Jenny had been upset, that was pretty evident. She had not even made any comment on Gina's invitation. She had seen Darius leave this morning and his step had been jaunty, his face content. He had waved, but in his hurry had not stopped to speak. What was going on, Gina wondered?

When Rachel came back, she was appalled to see the state that Jenny was in. "Jenny, what has happened to you?" she said, dropping to her knees beside her distraught sister.

"Let's just say that I made a disastrous mistake, one that won't happen again," Jenny said, quietly. The finality in her tone, made Rachel decide not to question her further.

Jenny had not left the flat or opened the shop for two days. She felt as though she was dying, and it was only when she saw her sister's distressed face that Jenny realised she could not wallow in her own misery like this. It wasn't fair to Rachel, so she began to go back down into the shop, although Jenny made no attempt at her designing. Her mind was not relaxed enough to cope with all the thought that was needed to put into it.

ɳ ɳ ɳ ɳ ɳ ɳ

Darius's meetings kept him occupied for two days and he fell into bed so late each night that there was no time to phone, but he had no idea of the heartache his absence would bring. He was secure in the knowledge that Jenny would have read the note and be waiting to see him as eagerly as he wanted to see her. When Darius arrived back home, he greeted his sister cheerfully, but his smile died as he observed her serious face.

"What is it, what's going on?"

"What have you done to Jenny?" Gina asked as she looked up at his concerned face.

"Nothing that she didn't want me to," he said, with a faint frown, as he stared at her.

"I think you'd better ring her as soon as possible," Gina said. "Because something is troubling her. She was a bit short with me when I spoke to her last."

"My next move, when I have a chance to put this briefcase down, was to do just that," Darius stated, pulling his mobile from his pocket. He became worried as he waited for an answer. Darius heard the phone ring, and the receiver was picked up, but as soon as he spoke, it was slammed down again. "Now what have I done?" Darius stared at the receiver as though it had just bitten him. Perhaps it was Rachel, another spat with James maybe. He rang again and was greeted with the same resounding thud. He felt his anger rise at Jenny's inexplicable behaviour.

After two days of this treatment, Darius began to get desperate. He had tried going to the flat, but his insistent ringing at the door brought no response. At first, he thought Jenny had gone away, but then realised with increasing anger and frustration that she was simply not answering the phone or door to him. His questions to Rachel when he did come across her with James were greeted with a curt, "You know what you've done, you... You!"

Rachel had turned away as though she could not bear to look at him, then flounced off. It hardly gave him the answer he required and even the amiable James had taken to giving him black looks. In the end, Darius gave up. Whatever he had done, Jenny must really hate him. He thought of the long-standing invitation to stay at a friend's villa in France and decided that now might be a good time to take him up on it. Darius needed to get right away out of this country and relax.

Chapter Twelve

As Darius lay on the beach soaking up the soothing warmth, a shadow came between him and the sun's rays and he squinted up, shielding his eyes. An extremely shapely dark-haired woman, wearing a minute bikini, stood gazing down at him appreciatively. She had noticed this large, handsome man walk down from the terrace of the villa next door, from the veranda of her own villa, and decided this new addition needed further investigation. She sauntered down on to the wide stretch of sand and drew her breath in as she approached him. Seeing him this close up and taking in his dark good looks and powerful body, the woman felt a surge of admiration, followed very closely by the stir of desire. Well, it would certainly do no harm to try her luck with this gorgeous specimen, she thought. She parted her lips in a seductive smile, showing small perfect white teeth.

"Hi, I'm your neighbour. I live just over there." She indicated, with a sweeping movement of one tanned arm, a large white villa partially hidden by a dense planting of shrubs and trees. "Jonathan often calls in for a drink, so please feel free to do the same, and my name is Marilyn, by the way."

Darius gazed up at the voluptuous woman and his lips twitched at her blatant flirting, as she hovered over him running her tongue over full red lips. "Really, what a pretty name."

When she had sauntered off with a wiggle of her hips, he stopped smiling abruptly. What the hell is wrong with me, Darius thought. I don't feel a thing and she is a very lovely woman. Shouldn't I at least have felt a vague attraction? He had politely turned down her invitation, it was obviously for more than just a drink, and had told her that he would not be staying very long. He had not even told her his name.

Darius lay still as Jenny's face filled his mind. You are driving me mad, he told her image. Stealing my heart is bad enough, but adding my mind to your trophies is unforgivable.

He mentioned his sultry visitor from the next-door villa to Jonathan, and his friend laughed knowingly. "I have only met her on one or two occasions, and that was along with a room full of party guests. Marilyn can be quite amusing, and there's no getting away from it, the woman is good to look at. She has a lot of male friends, barely tolerates females, they might present a threat, but if you are in need, and I don't mean sexually, she can be relied on to help. Mind you, it's usually men who sing her praises, so it could be a bit biased."

ൡ ൡ ൡ ൡ ൡ ൡ

The view from his friend's villa was tranquil and beautiful, and Darius sat on the terrace gazing at the neat rows of vines that ran as far as the eye could see, disappearing over the hills and around the patches of woodland which impeded their progress. Jonathan sat opposite him, with his head buried in a newspaper, totally absorbed. Probably the financial pages, Darius mused, as he studied his friend with renewed interest. He was a good-looking man, yet had never settled down. Maybe he had just not found the right person. Apart from work, I wonder what he does with his time, Darius pondered.

As though he suddenly became aware of his scrutiny, Jonathan slowly looked up, and folding his paper, threw it down onto the table. "Okay, what's with all this guarded silence? Obviously, a woman is at the bottom of it all."

"Why should it be a woman?" Darius blustered. "Couldn't I simply just need a holiday? You know, just get away, a welcome break from the rat race."

"Whatever you care to call it, I have been there my friend, trodden that same stony path, and a holiday will not cure it, believe me." His friend cast him an old-fashioned look.

Darius stared at him in surprise, Jonathan had been smiling, but the sadness in his eyes had given him away and he was still suffering deeply by the look of it. "Anybody I know?" Darius enquired.

"Never you mind," Jonathan flushed. "Anyway, it was not her fault, she never gave me a second glance, it was completely one-sided."

It was the flush that did it and a suspicion formed in Darius's mind. He remembered on one of Jonathan's last visits to England when he had come to stay with them, how animated Gina had been, and how quiet and withdrawn she had appeared after he had gone. At the time, being slightly younger, Darius had dismissed her mood as part of the vagaries of women. Now he realised that perhaps Jonathan's love was not as one-sided as his friend thought. Well perhaps fate could be given a slight nudge in the right direction, and when he got back, he must remember to invite him over. Darius smiled thoughtfully at Jonathan.

"Why are you giving me that calculating look, Darius?" His friend stared at him warily.

"No reason," he said breezily. "Just a passing thought."

Jonathan was still giving him a suspicious look and Darius blinked, gazing back at him innocently, then changed the subject.

ﬔﬔﬔﬔﬔﬔ

The days passed, the weather was balmy, Jonathan was good company, and yet Darius was unable to relax. He found his mind returning again and again to Jenny, remembering the soft inviting feel of her. He visualised her cascade of curls on the pillow, her parted lips, and he cursed his inability to forget her. The nights were the worst, his sleep was fitful, and Darius often sat propped up against the pillows, trying to immerse himself in some of the interesting books at hand. In the end, he got fed up with reading the same passages over and over again, and gave up in disgust, pacing agitatedly about the room instead.

Even Jonathan started to become exasperated with Darius's constant nocturnal activities. "You're even keeping me awake now," his friend protested. He pointed out that the floorboards in the old villa were worn and tended to creak, especially when heavy bodies constantly walked about on them, disturbing other residents.

"There's only you here," Darius pointed out, with an attempt at humour.

Jonathan folded his arms and narrowed his eyes at the other man. "Will you please go home, Darius? Clear up whatever problem you thought that you had left behind and give me some peace. You will be welcome back, naturally."

An hour later Jonathan sat on the bed feeling guilty at his ultimatum and watched while his friend packed his travel bag. "You didn't have to take me up on it so soon, Darius."

"Don't worry about it, Jonathan. Besides, you're right. I have to sort my life out, because I can't go on like this. Feeling so down is bad enough, inflicting it on others is totally out of order."

"Are you going to be all right, my friend?"

"Why shouldn't I be?" Darius said shortly, then sighed apologetically as he glanced at his friend's concerned face, saying quietly. "I will be fine, Jonathan, please don't give it another thought."

Darius wished that he could clear up his problem as easily as his friend thought, but he couldn't, and this was something he would have to live with. He was determined to push Jenny to the back of his mind.

Chapter Thirteen

Gradually, as time passed, Jenny's tension eased and Darius stopped being the dominant factor in her thoughts, at least for part of the day. She was able to regain her cheerful good humour, even accepting a couple of invitations from Jason, and life resumed an air of normality.

One morning when Jenny woke, she felt strange, slightly nauseous, and a nasty suspicion entered her mind. She had been so immersed in her misery that she hadn't realised her body wasn't following its normal cycle. Jenny felt frightened and alarmed to even contemplate what was becoming glaringly obvious. She did not confide in Rachel, as she wanted to be absolutely sure. How could she have been so stupid? Then one morning the problem was over as suddenly as it had arisen. As soon as she woke up Jenny knew that something was desperately wrong, cramping pains in her stomach made her scramble out of bed and into the bathroom. She knew now that there would be no baby to complicate her life.

Jenny had cried with worry when she had first thought herself pregnant, now as she staggered into her bedroom and threw herself onto the bed, she cried with grief. She wept until she felt totally drained, until her throat and chest ached, and her eyes were so swollen that she could hardly see. Jenny had not wanted to carry a child, but deep inside she had wanted to keep this small part of Darius, and now even that had been snatched away. Jenny put her hands over her face as though to stem the flood of tears that would not be contained, but they trickled through her fingers and dropped off her chin into her hair, forming a spreading stain on her pillow.

Rachel, drawn to her room by the heart-rending whimpers of distress, was horrified to find her sister in such a state. "Jenny, oh, God! Jenny, what is it?" She put her arms around her sister, pulling her up and cradling her protectively.

Jenny told her haltingly, her voice breaking on occasion, what had happened. It took a long time between bouts of sobbing for Rachel to drag it from her, and she was as weepy as Jenny was when she had finished. Jenny felt as though she had suffered a bereavement.

"And so you have," Rachel stated. She felt almost as upset as Jenny "Now please, Jen, try and get some rest and leave work alone for a while."

"It's so silly," Jenny said tearfully. "It hardly even had a chance to grow."

Rachel just hugged her harder and as the tears welled up again, her own eyes filled. Later in the day, she persuaded Jenny to visit the doctors and make sure that all was normal. Rachel was only reassured when she accompanied her and heard his opinion herself on the condition of Jenny's health, but it was the state of her sister's mind that really troubled her. Rachel began to get seriously worried about Jenny. Her sister had lost weight, and no matter what tempting food was placed in front of her, she only picked uninterestedly at it. She had also taken to shutting herself in her bedroom and would just lie brooding, with silent tears coursing down her face. In the end, a growing awareness of the misery she was causing her sister helped Jenny to try and snap out of her downward spiral of depression. She made an effort to eat more of the food that Rachel took such care and trouble to prepare for her.

꒰ ꒱ ꒰ ꒱ ꒰ ꒱

Darius returned from his sojourn abroad feeling refreshed and in a more positive frame of mind. His forced cheerfulness worried Gina even more than his morose mood had done before. It was as though he was pretending that Jenny didn't exist. If her name was mentioned, he reacted by immediately changing the subject, his face set and unapproachable.

As he settled back into the pattern of work, his restlessness returned, and his associates wished fervently that Darius would go away again. At home, the sight of Rachel, on her occasional visits, only served to remind him of the woman he wanted so much to forget, and gradually his black mood returned.

"Uh-oh!" quipped Dominic. "Doctor Jekyll has vanished and Mr Hyde has returned, I see."

They jumped as Darius slammed the library door to shut their laughter out, but Gina only gave a faint smile. She felt far more concerned about the way Darius was sinking into depression than her brothers were.

She opened the library door tentatively. "Darius, this is getting beyond a joke."

He scowled at her and curtly told her to leave him alone.

"No! Darius, I won't. You are creating a terrible atmosphere in the house. You even snapped at Gran the other day and she looked quite hurt. Everyone is fed up with you, and you had better get your act together before father blows his top."

Darius blinked, trying to remember when he had insulted his grandmother, and his poor father had enough on his plate trying to manage Isabel without him making things worse, he thought tiredly.

Gina stood behind him and put her hands on his shoulders. "Let's go out for the evening. You need a change."

"I don't want to go anywhere." He shrugged, uninterestedly.

"Oh, come on, Darius. That new place has opened in town, and I have been dying to try it out, but I need an escort. James tells me that the food is fabulous. Please?" she wheedled.

"You win, you persistent pest." Darius let his breath out in a reluctant chuckle. "You are a very domineering woman. Did anyone ever tell you that?"

"Yes," she giggled. "Constantly."

Gina grabbed his arm, as though he might change his mind, snatched her bag up as she hustled him out of the door, and then marched him to his car.

ריריריריריר

The evening had hardly been a resounding success, Gina thought as she lay in her bed later that night. It had started out well enough, until she had tried to steer the subject around to the touchy matter of Jenny. One thing had led to another, and they had ended up in a slanging match. Darius had been starting to get quite insulting, and her own temper had risen to match his. Her final shot had been. "You useless wimp. You are sad, do you know that, and Jenny is far better off without you!"

It was as though Gina had held a match to his touch paper, Darius leapt up white-faced, sending his chair crashing over to the floor. "What the bloody hell do you know about it, just keep your pathetic thoughts to yourself, and in future stay out of my affairs," he roared. Then Darius had stormed out, leaving a sea of astounded faces behind him.

Gina had sunk down in her seat with hot cheeks, trying to make herself look inconspicuous. Well, she thought, that was probably better left unsaid. What shall I do for an encore? She felt even worse when a hovering waiter stood the chair upright and slid it back under the table with a polite smile. At that point, Gina hastily scuttled away from the curious gazes that followed her from the room.

Matters had deteriorated since the unfortunate altercation in the restaurant, and most days when he wasn't at work, Darius had taken to shutting himself away in the library. Gina was listening outside the door. She was more worried about him than ever and even his brothers were now beginning to take it a bit more seriously. They stood in the hallway talking together with her in subdued voices.

Darius was totally unaware of the concerned whispers outside the door. He was slumped in his chair, sunk in a black despair, when a sudden thought occurred to him that galvanised him into action. He had to make Jenny see him. His sudden appearance caused an uncomfortable silence, not that they needed to worry about his reaction to them standing there, because Darius pushed through as though he hadn't seen them, and was striding out of the front door before they could even find their voices again.

Jenny still felt washed out but was coming to terms with her loss. She was starting to interest herself in her designs again and had taken to going for long walks along the local footpaths. One evening, just as she was getting ready to leave for one of these walks, the doorbell rang. She made her way tiredly towards the door, opening it with the chain on. Jenny was shocked to find herself staring into a pair of dark eyes, which looked equally as tired as her own.

"Darius," she breathed, then pulled herself together, and asked coldly. "What do you want?"

"Please let me in, we have to talk."

"No! We don't. Go away." Jenny stared at him lifelessly. Then she closed the door.

"If you don't open this bloody door, I will break it down." Darius thumped hard on it.

"Say what you have to say and make it quick, I'm going out," Jenny snapped, opening it so suddenly, that he nearly fell in.

Darius pushed past her and planted himself in the middle of the room. He suddenly seemed to be at a loss for words, as he gazed hungrily at her.

"Well?" she queried, tiredly.

"Are you all right?" he asked abruptly. Darius had a faint flush on his cheekbones and Jenny looked up at him in surprise.

"Of course I'm all right. Why shouldn't I be?"

"I wondered if there might have been any unfortunate repercussions from our, ah, encounter." Darius cleared his throat and looked down at his feet.

She felt such anger and pain that Jenny thought she would explode. and for a moment, could not speak. "The unfortunate repercussion, as you call it, decided that this was not such a good place to be, and left in rather a hurry." Her voice broke, as she remembered the strangely empty feeling she had been left with.

He whitened and took a step towards her, but Jenny put her hand up, warningly. "Don't! Stay right away from me."

"I just wanted to know, that's all. If there had been a problem, I wanted to make it right." Darius held his own hands out appealingly.

"How much would it have cost?" she sneered, as her head jerked up.

His anger was almost tangible at such a suggestion, and Jenny took a halting step backwards.

"Money does not come into it. I was prepared to marry you, I did not want any child of mine growing up without me there," Darius raged.

Jenny stared at him miserably, knowing that she would never have seen him again if he had not thought she may be pregnant. "There is now no problem, so no complications to ensnare you," she said quietly. "Now, please leave me alone to get on with my life." How could he dismiss Melissa so easily like this, Jenny thought.

Darius stared at her forlorn face, wanting to hold her to him, and soothe her troubles away, wanting to shout that he wished there had been complications. He needed a reason for her to want him around, but obviously, Jenny didn't want any part of him. His unfortunate way of putting into words what he would like to do had put paid to any feelings she may have had. Darius sighed in despair and moved slowly towards the door, then he hesitated and turned.

"Take care of yourself, Jenny, you don't look well, and you're looking way too thin." He let his eyes wander over her, drinking in the sight of her, and then he let himself out. Darius sat in his car and ran his broad hand through his thick dark hair tiredly. He thought of home, but it held no appeal. Darius felt like a lovesick fool. He had never thought of himself as a family man, yet now his heart grieved for the tiny lost being that he could have loved so much. His heart also ached for Jenny and his life would be empty without her in it. Business, which had consumed so much of his time, now seemed to have lost its importance, and Darius felt trapped in an inner loneliness.

ּ ּ ּ ּ ּ ּ

Rachel's affair, meanwhile, was flourishing, and James kept pressing her to name a date. "He's serious, Jen. He really loves me, and he's proposed. I must say that the prospect of being related to Isabel is a bit daunting though, and his older brothers are so overpowering, aren't they?" She stopped, "Oh, Jen, I'm sorry."

"Don't be so silly, Rachel, you can't avoid talking about the man that you are going to marry forever, you know." Jenny smiled wanly. "Life goes on, as they say, and I am slowly getting over Darius. I'm pleased for you and James, I really am. As to his family, it's James you're marrying, not them, and it's really only Isabel who is the main problem. You would not believe one woman could be such a pain, would you?"

"It's all so furtive, somehow," Rachel sighed. "Having to wait for her to go away before we can spend time at the house."

"Rachel, have you given any consideration as to where you and James are going to live?" Jenny gazed at her sister questioningly.

"Oh, lord, we haven't even begun to discuss that, and I suppose we must." Her sister sat up straight with a startled look on her face as reality sank in. "There is no way that we could settle in with his parents." Rachel chuckled as she conjured up Isabel's outraged face if she thought that they were thinking of moving in with her. Jenny laughed with her, as she shared the joke.

Jenny settled down into a routine. Her concentration soon improved, and she was able to take up her designing again as the ideas gradually began to flow. Her folder rapidly began to fill with new samples, and in the end, she had so many, that she decided it was about time she took them to one of her London outlets. Jenny gathered her designs together and made ready for her trip. She would make a long day of it and splash out on a few new outfits. It was not often that she made the effort to go on a shopping spree.

On one of her previous trips to London, Jenny had bumped into another young designer in the doorway of a small company, one that supplied a regular source of income for her. They had laughingly apologised, taking an instant liking to each other. Her fellow designer's name was Judith, and she was a friendly girl, with a bubbly strong-minded personality. She was short and plump, yet very feminine, and had large round brown eyes that reminded Jenny of an owl, albeit a pretty one, and her large glasses added to the overall impression. She had fair hair scraped up into an untidy bun, which despite the straggly wisps hanging over her face, looked very attractive. Now whenever they met after completing their business transactions, they had formed the habit of lunching together and most of their time was spent on talking about design.

Jenny chose a day that she knew her friend would be visiting one of the same companies and arranged to meet with her. This time when she saw Judith, her friend was alighting from a taxi with a pile of folders that were sliding out of her arms, with the contents threatening to spill out onto the pavement. Jenny ran forward, and hitching her own folder awkwardly over one shoulder, began to help Judith with her burdens.

"Oh, thanks so much, Jenny, an extra pair of hands is very welcome right at this moment," she said with breathless gratitude. "You would think that I'd be better organised by now, but I always seem to bring far too much work every time I travel up."

When they had completed their various transactions, they left together to find a place to have their lunch. They found a reasonably quiet restaurant tucked away in one of the numerous small streets that ran off the main road they had to pass through. Once they had settled at the table and decided on their order, they both sat back with a simultaneous sigh of relief and exchanged a laugh at their mutual satisfaction.

"If we weren't in such a public place," Judith groaned, "I would kick my shoes off. My feet are absolutely killing me." She reached down and massaged one of her ankles.

"Never mind about that," Jenny interrupted. "What were you doing with all those folders? You must have worked like a Trojan to get that lot churned out."

"You heartless woman," Judith said, straightening up and taking a sip of her tea. "Not a word about my poor feet."

"I feel your pain," Jenny said, with a titter, adding impatiently. "Well?"

"That was sympathy?" Judith raised her brows, then shrugged and explained. "Oh, well, you know, I was not that marvellous a designer, and my ideas were not quite what they wanted. I found that I was much better at selling other people's work. In fact, I am very good, and if I say so myself, my powers of persuasion are gaining quite a reputation."

"So, you take other people's designs and tote them around the various companies, do you?" Jenny asked with growing interest.

"I do," Judith looked smug. "Actually, I am now a registered agent and doing very nicely, thank you."

"Congratulations," Jenny smiled.

"I could act for you, if you like. My charges are reasonable and for a friend, I would certainly lower them." Her friend frowned at her thoughtfully. Judith raised her eyebrows inquiringly at Jenny, but before the other girl could answer, the waitress came with their meal, so they paused while she set it down, made sure they were happy with the food, and then departed.

"It's very nice of you to offer, and I will give it some serious thought." Jenny smiled at Judith. "I have to admit that sometimes the journey can be real nuisance, and I don't always feel like tramping from one place to another. Just let me think about it for a while."

"You know, your designs would go down well in France." Judith studied her, head on one side and blinked owlishly at her.

"Are you serious?" Jenny stared at her. "It's hard enough to get going here, let alone another country."

"The opportunities are better over there. In fact, I have to travel over again in ten days' time. Have you heard of 'Charrier', the interior designer?" Judith asked. At Jenny's blank face, she laughed. "Well, perhaps not, you don't travel much, do you? Anyway, it is quite an exclusive furnishing establishment, and they like to have their own designers. My boyfriend Gerard designs for them and also buys in patterns from other new designers," Judith added persuasively. "I'm sure that yours would appeal. Why don't you come with me?"

"Over to France?" Jenny was taken aback.

"Why not, it would do you good. You do look a little pale, if I may say so, and apart from anything else, think of all those lovely men." Judith insisted, leaning forward eagerly. At the shuttered look which immediately appeared on her friend's face, she said. "Ah! Had some recent trouble, have you? I recognise that look; it's the same one that I have seen in my own mirror from time to time."

"I would rather not talk about it," Jenny said, with a small grimace. "In fact, I don't even want to think about it."

"Take no notice of me, I shall not probe. I can bite my tongue on the odd occasion," Judith laughed apologetically. "Just give my offer some thought. We can stay at Gerard's apartment; it has plenty of spare rooms. You have my number, give me a ring when you've made your mind up."

"What about Gerard, won't he mind?" Jenny queried.

"Oh, no, Gerard lives over here a good deal of the time. We share a flat in Chelsea. The apartment in Paris is simply there for convenience. I often stay in it by myself when I go over to drop designs off."

"I thought you said that Gerard brought the designs?" Jenny looked puzzled.

"He does when he is there, and of course, you could just show them to him here, but think of the fun you could have with me in Paris. As it happens, his partner Maurice is based there all the time. He buys the designs that I take over while Gerard is busy here."

When they had finished their lunch, Jenny began to think more seriously about her friend's offer. The thought of travelling somewhere totally different appealed strongly to her, Judith was good company, and she did need a break. Even before they parted, Jenny had made her mind up.

"I would love to come with you, Judith, it will be something new and exciting to look forward to. Thank you so much for asking me."

"My pleasure," beamed her friend. "Having you along will give me a chance to show off the Paris that I know. Don't worry about travel arrangements, I will take care of everything, just remember to bring your passport. Oh, and some money to treat yourself with."

Jenny was envious of Judith's capable confidence and left her with a lightness in her step that had been missing for quite some while. She wished that she could organise her own life as well as Judith had. Her friend seemed content and fulfilled with her lot and according to the rapturous description of Gerard that Judith had monopolised the rest of the conversation with, he was a god amongst men. Jenny hoped for her sake that he lived up to Judith's high opinion of him.

Chapter Fourteen

Rachel was relieved to hear of Jenny's plans. This was just the sort of tonic her sister needed, and when the time came for Jenny's departure, Rachel felt as excited as her sister did. She helped her to pack, and in her enthusiasm put far too many things into the case, mostly clothes that her sister didn't want.

"Rachel! Will you please stop fussing over me? Now I've got to repack all my things again, you've muddled them all up." Jenny immediately took them out again, sighing with exasperation as she frowned at her sister.

Rachel grimaced apologetically. "Sorry, Jen, I am just so anxious that you take everything you need. You want at least one glamorous dress, and you never know who you might meet." Rachel held up the pretty dress that Jenny had thrown aside and then stopped talking as she saw the impatient glance that her sister cast at her.

"I am not," Jenny emphasised, "Looking to impress men, if that is what's on your mind." She began to carefully repack, folding a few sensible clothes neatly into her case.

Rachel watched on with disappointment. "Oh, Jen, surely one evening dress wouldn't be overdoing it."

"Actually, if you must know, I plan to do some shopping while I'm over there, so if anything more glitzy is required, I can go and buy it." Jenny smiled at her sister's downcast face. "Does that satisfy you?"

"Sure does," Rachel brightened. "I don't want my sister looking dull and drab, especially when you go to this 'Charrier' interview."

"Don't worry, I'll do my best to impress. Anyway, it's my work they want to see, not how I dress," stressed Jenny.

The doorbell rang and Rachel rushed to let James in. He had volunteered to take them to the airport, as Rachel was adamant that she must be there to see her sister off. Jenny was, in fact, grateful to have the reassurance of their company, as she was feeling nervous at the thought of the journey and had been dreading the ride alone to the terminal.

When they reached their destination, Jenny persuaded her sister to leave her at the entrance. Judith would be waiting for her inside the terminal, and she knew that James had planned to take Rachel away again, so they would need to get back and do their own packing. It wouldn't hurt to leave the shop closed for a week, and her sister would be back after a few days, so there was nothing to worry about.

"Are you sure that you'll be all right on your own? I feel guilty about leaving you like this." Rachel regarded her with concern.

"I'll be fine, honestly," Jenny said with more confidence than she felt. "Judith is around here somewhere, so off you go and enjoy yourselves."

"If you're sure you'll be all right," her sister said, anxiously.

"Of course I will. See what happens when you come to see me off? You would think that I was going away forever." Jenny gulped, with a faint smile, as she hugged James and shed a few tears when Rachel pulled her close.

Jenny felt apprehensive as she entered the airport. She had never flown before and yet it was not that which made her nervous. It was the thought of being in a foreign country. To a lot of people that might seem ridiculous in this day and age, but for Jenny this was all new and overwhelming. and yet a sense of excitement was surfacing and beginning to overcome the apprehension. Jenny felt exhilarated as she stood among the bustling travellers, and looked around trying to get her bearings, then her eyes connected with a familiar face as she found Judith hovering anxiously near the check-in desk.

When she saw Jenny appear, a look of relief crossed the other girl's face. "Thank God, I was worried in case you had a last-minute change of heart."

"Oh, I'm not late, am I?" Jenny gave her a look of concern. "You know I would have let you know if I had changed my mind. I wouldn't just stand you up."

"I know, take no notice of me, I always get a bit tense when I'm travelling." Judith patted her arm. "Now let me take you over and introduce you to Gerard. He's waiting for us in the coffee lounge. He always insists on seeing me off."

Jenny was surprised and amused to see that 'this god amongst men,' was short and slim, with fair slicked-back hair and a shy manner. It was when he smiled and spoke that she saw his attraction and charm. Gerard's face lit up, his blue eyes sparkled, and his accent sounded gorgeous. By the time the announcement for the departure came, Jenny felt as though she had known him all her life and that she had gained a friend. She also now knew all about his family, particularly about his brother Maurice, who sounded like a real Romeo. Someone Jenny decided that she would rather not meet.

"He's not as bad as he's painted," Judith giggled. "Gerard always exaggerates his reputation."

"So, he has got one?" Jenny laughed.

"Well, yes," Judith grinned. "Just not that bad."

Jenny felt a sense of trepidation as she boarded the plane and sank down into her seat with a quickly beating heart. As they took off and her body was pressed back into the seat, she was consumed by a momentary fear and grabbed at the hand that Judith kindly offered. Afterwards, as she calmed down, Jenny felt obliged to apologise to her friend for the nail marks she had left in her hand.

"Remind me to wear tough gloves on the return journey." Judith rubbed at them with a rueful laugh. "Now take a look out of the window and see what you're missing."

Jenny tentatively peered down on the ever-decreasing patchwork quilt below, and drew her breath in. "The houses and fields look so tiny; they don't look quite real."

Jenny was extremely glad she had taken Judith up on her offer. If she saw nothing else, this alone was worth the trip. No doubt Judith was blasé about these journeys now, but for Jenny, it was a tremendous new experience, and one that she was fully appreciating.

She actually felt disappointed when they landed and yet, at the same time, was glad to get her feet back onto solid ground. Even the journey from the airport by taxi to Gerard's apartment filled her with a growing sense of excitement, as she sat with her nose pressed against the half-open window eagerly breathing in the atmosphere of Paris. She ignored the fumes thrown up by the interweaving cars, wondering how they managed to miss each other.

When they arrived at Gerard's home, Jenny was amazed at the size of the place and wandered around feeling slightly bemused. For some reason she had been expecting a small cosy flat, not this huge rambling apartment. Jenny stopped and gazed out of the large double windows of the living room, which opened out onto a small wrought iron balcony hanging precariously over the pretty square below. Jenny stepped out cautiously, and she sighed in pleasure when on peering down, a small café caught her eye, making a promise to herself that one of the first things she would do in the morning would be to sit at one of those little tables placed neatly outside its doors and enjoy a cup of coffee.

As Jenny unpacked, she felt contentment wash over her. At long last she was well away from the source of all her troubles, and she felt totally relaxed. When Jenny had finished putting her clothes away, she wandered back into the spacious sitting room and found her friend reclining on one of the large comfortable chairs, with her feet up on a small footstool. "There you are," Judith said. "I've poured you a nice cool drink, now sit and enjoy."

"Thank you, Judith, just what I needed," Jenny smiled, as she accepted the glass and took a sip, then raised her brows. "This is wine!"

"Of course it is. How else would one celebrate arriving in France?" She raised the glass in a toast. "May your stay be rewarding and all your troubles disappear."

"I'll drink to that." Jenny sank down on one of the sumptuous-looking chairs and raised her own glass. "If only life was that simple, I would drink all the time."

They smiled at each other happily, sipping slowly at the mellow wine and just enjoying the moment. Judith finished first and put her glass down, becoming all businesslike. "Right, let me outline our itinerary for tomorrow." Jenny raised her brows at her friend, who had the grace to laugh ruefully. "I know, I know. I've taken over again. Sorry. Honestly, though, you will like what I've arranged. First, we will present your designs at Maurice's workrooms, then we will go on for lunch at a very exclusive hotel. I promise that you will be quite impressed by it. Then we will stop thinking of work, go out on the town and have a good time just browsing. The shops here are absolutely fabulous."

"It makes me feel tired just contemplating it." Jenny said, her mind whirling with all these plans.

"That's just the result of the plane journey, and you're not used to the experience," Judith stated. "Go and enjoy a relaxing bath and get yourself an early night. I've got some phone calls to make and then I shall be going off to bed myself."

Jenny took her friend at her word and had a long, leisurely soak, almost falling asleep in the deep old-fashioned tub, and she was grateful to snuggle down in the extremely comfortable bed at the end of what had been a tiring but exciting day.

ƝƝƝƝƝƝ

The morning found Jenny comfortably seated, as she had promised herself, at one of the small tables in the square, sipping coffee and nibbling contentedly on a croissant. She was profoundly relieved to find that the waiter could speak some English, as her schoolgirl attempt at the French language left much to be desired and had left them both laughing helplessly as she stumbled to a halt. Jenny was, for the first time in a long while, feeling that all was well with her world. She gazed around, admiring the beautiful fountain that resided in the middle of the old square, and watched as the water bubbled over the top tier, sparkling in the sunlight as it cascaded down into the basin below. Jenny sat listening to the soft splashing sound appreciatively. It had a strangely calming effect on her.

A man obscured her view, and she waited impatiently for him to move away. When he did not, Jenny shaded her eyes and peered up at him with a curious frown.

He smiled down at her; a practiced smile, and said with a strong French accent, "You are in need of some company, Mademoiselle?"

"No, thank you." Jenny smiled politely back.

"You will not be sorry, and I make stimulating conversation." He looked hurt and puzzled. "Why would you give up this wonderful opportunity to get to know me?"

She found herself laughing at him, despite her intention to snub him, and gave a small helpless nod of agreement. "I suppose it won't do me any harm to share a cup of coffee with you, Monsieur."

He seated himself opposite Jenny, giving her a flirtatious look. As he turned to order coffee, Jenny studied him furtively. He was reasonably good-looking, with thick brown hair, twinkling brown eyes and a positively dazzling smile. His charm lay in his manner, a fact of which he was very well aware.

"Why are you alone, a beautiful woman such as you?" He leaned forward with a smouldering look and Jenny laughed, she could not help it, he sounded so corny.

"I'm sorry," she said contritely, as he sat back looking wounded, and Jenny cleared her throat. "That was rude of me."

She stared at him. Surely, she was not supposed to take him seriously?

He stared back and his lips curled in a humorous smile. "I tease you, ma chérie. Let me introduce myself. I am Maurice Charrier. Judith told me that you were here. I save you a journey, yes?"

Jenny was totally thrown by this information. Surely the great man himself had not come here just to see her? Then she collected her wits. Of course he hadn't, that would be too ridiculous. Jenny looked at him in confusion and at her puzzled look, Maurice enlarged on the subject. "Did not Judith tell you? I have an adjoining apartment, and I came to collect some work I had left behind. I decided to pay Judith a courtesy call and while I was there, she took the opportunity to show me your work. I am most impressed." He sat back, regarding her with appreciative eyes. "Not only beautiful, talented also, it seems."

"Thank you. Did you really like my designs?" Jenny asked eagerly, blushing at the disturbing gleam in his eyes.

"I have said so," he nodded. "I will take them and would be pleased to be shown more of your talented ideas."

Jenny was thrilled and slightly overawed to think that sitting opposite her was 'the Maurice Charrier', head of the company that bore his name.

"Do not look so alarmed." He laughed sympathetically. "I am as human as you are, as you see. You wish to touch me and find out if I speak the truth?"

Maurice held his hands out, inviting her to look more closely, and Jenny fanned her flushed cheeks. She would give touching him a miss, because she had a feeling that to do so would be a mistake.

"I am so embarrassed. I thought that you were making a pass at me," she said honestly.

"But of course I was," he grinned, mischievously. "Have you not noticed that I am a very good-looking guy, and you are a beautiful lady? A match made in heaven, oui?"

"Well, thank you for the compliment." Jenny laughed at his audacity and humour.

"Again, I speak the truth." He smiled at her pink face. "I have decided that you will have the privilege of dining with me tonight."

She stared at him, not sure what to say. Judith may have made plans for tonight, yet he was an important buyer, and Jenny could not afford to ignore him.

Maurice saw the indecision on her face and leaned forward, saying wickedly, "Consider this blackmail, mademoiselle. You do wish your designs to be taken and printed by my company, do you not?"

"You are dreadful, and you don't mean a word of it," Jenny giggled.

"I am very serious," he said softly. "At least about the meal. Will you do me the honour?"

Jenny found his light-hearted company amusing and decided to take him up on his offer, but she would have to square it with Judith first, of course. She smiled shyly across at him. "I would love to share a meal with you, that is if I still have the strength left after Judith has dragged me all around the shops in Paris."

"Ah! Judith." He rolled his eyes expressively. "She is full of life that one, and the minx leads my brother a merry dance."

Jenny looked at him with growing enlightenment. Am I particularly obtuse? she thought, wondering why she had not connected him with Gerard before. Jenny could not remember if Judith had even mentioned her boyfriend's surname, yet looking at Maurice she could now see the strong resemblance. For some reason, she had not connected him with the Maurice that Judith had spoken of.

"I'm sorry, I didn't realise that you two were brothers," Jenny said. "I don't recall Judith ever mentioning it. Although she probably did, but I was so up in the air at the thought of coming over here, that I could easily have missed it."

"No matter, you know now," he dismissed, lightly. "I would also like to show you Paris and it will be at a slower pace, I can assure you."

When she left him, it was with a decided spring in her step. There was something about Maurice that made her feel bubbly and totally feminine. Not that she was drawn to him physically. Jenny was under no illusions about Maurice. He was a consummate flirt, yet he made her feel good about herself, and she was determined to enjoy her evening with him.

Maurice watched her leave with speculative eyes, he felt odd, a mixture of his usual heady desire for a beautiful woman and something more. He had never felt like this before. It was too soon to be love, of course, yet he felt the danger signals.

He would have to tread warily around this little spider. Maurice had the unsettling feeling that it would be all too easy to become entangled in her silken web.

Judith glanced up from a folder as Jenny let herself in, noting Jenny's happy face and flushed cheeks. "Hi! Have a nice time? Sexy, isn't he?" she laughed. "I hope you didn't mind me telling him where to find you, I knew you would find his company stimulating. At least it's saved us a trip to his workrooms, and it will give us more time for all those lovely shops."

Jenny smiled as she told her of Maurice's invitation and sat down, feeling slightly breathless. "Unless you have got something else planned? I can always cancel."

"Nonsense! You go and have a good time," Judith stated firmly. She gazed at Jenny thoughtfully. "Hmm, this means, of course, that you will have to buy something fabulous to wear. He's bound to take you somewhere really exclusive." Judith closed the folder and pushed it aside, jumping up and instructing Jenny to get her purse and jacket. "Come on," she enthused. "Let's go and spend your money on some gorgeous clothes, get something that will knock his eyes out."

"I don't want to give him the wrong idea," Jenny laughed. "Just something dressy will do."

Judith, as she had feared, walked her to a standstill and persuaded her to buy far too many clothes. Jenny felt as though she had been caught up in a whirlwind and was exhausted when they finally made it back to the apartment, yet she had still thoroughly enjoyed her day, despite the hectic rush. They threw themselves into the comfortable chairs and put their feet up, sighing with exhaustion.

"Are you trying to kill me?" Jenny groaned, as she leaned her head back tiredly. "Please tell me that we are not going to keep this hectic pace up."

"Relax," Judith giggled tiredly. "I'm always like this on the first day here. I become less manic with time."

"Right, I'm going to see what I actually bought," Jenny sat up slowly, smiling. 'You had me in such a whirl that I hardly realised what purchases I made."

ꐦ ꐦ ꐦ ꐦ ꐦ

"What shall I wear?" Jenny pondered as she spread her new wardrobe out on the bed. She gazed in bewilderment at the varied selection of glamorous dresses and called out. "Did you really persuade me to buy all these?"

Judith staggered in tiredly, leaning against the door frame, and frowned thoughtfully as she studied them. "How about that green one?" She indicated a shimmering deep green dress. "It's absolutely gorgeous, I liked it as soon as you tried it on."

Jenny picked the dress up and held it against her body, turning and looking at herself in the mirror. For a moment she closed her eyes, as a strong dark face intruded into her thoughts and Jenny remembered the last time she had worn such a slinky glamorous dress. She slipped the dress on. "What do you think?"

"That looks terrific. It does something to your eyes. They look sort of deep green and mysterious." Judith tipped her head to one side and stood gazing admiringly at Jenny. "That should wow him all right!"

"Do you think it's a bit too clingy?" Jenny asked, as her friend's voice brought her back to the present. She felt a touch of dismay, as she continued to stare at her reflection critically.

"Oh, for goodness sake, it's perfectly fine on you. I wish I could wear something that sexy. I can imagine my lumps and bumps compressed into that. Not pretty." Judith sat on the bed and regarded Jenny with envious good humour.

"You know very well that the men would go wild with lust at the amount of flesh you would expose," Jenny laughed.

Judith giggled as she looked down at herself admiringly. She had a large bust and was used to men talking at it rather than to her, whenever she made conversation with them. She accepted the fact that Gerard had first been drawn to her because of her attributes, but as he had got to know Judith more intimately, he had fallen in love with her and now to him her figure was just a bonus. It was her personality that had finally captured him.

ഇ ഇ ഇ ഇ ഇ ഇ

Jenny had taken great care with her appearance and knew that she looked her best. Judith was right, the dress did flatter her. It looked good. She twirled in front of the mirror, until Judith's voice from the doorway halted her childish antics.

"I told you that it would look fabulous on you."

"I do look great, if I say so myself," Jenny boasted. "And you were right again; it pays to splash out on a few good quality clothes."

She took one last look in the mirror, trying to subdue her curls before she hastened to answer the ring at the door. Jenny felt confident and feminine as she opened it, and the feeling was further enhanced as she observed the arrested expression on Maurice's face.

"Is this vision of loveliness before me real?" he breathed, looking down at her with appreciative eyes.

She blushed, thrown by his amorous glances. Then Jenny laughed, as she saw the mischievous twinkle in his eye. "And is this extremely handsome guy really my escort?"

They smiled at each other in mutual admiration. "Go on, you two, have a good time," Judith beamed, as she waved them off. She shut the door and leaned against it thoughtfully. She had caught the fleeting expression of vulnerability on Maurice's face and hoped that he would not get too serious about Jenny. Judith sensed that the other girl would not give her heart lightly and having once given it, could not easily forget that love. She shrugged, Maurice was an inveterate flirt, he could handle it. At least she hoped so, for his sake.

Chapter Fifteen

Jenny felt cherished, happy, and positively glowed as she leaned back in her chair. The restaurant was as Judith had predicted, exclusive, and Maurice was an attentive and attractive companion. She smiled softly at him, her eyes sparkling with excitement. "Thank you so much for this, Maurice."

"It is my pleasure, chérie, and I am a much-envied man." He smiled back, with twinkling eyes, as he observed her innocent enjoyment. At her perplexed look, Maurice glanced around, lifting his hand in a sweeping gesture. "Do you not see the many admiring eyes fixed upon you? They wonder what I have done to deserve one such as you."

He sat back and let his eyes wander over her curves. Jenny looked truly breathtaking tonight. The low-cut green dress had thin straps holding it up, exposing soft creamy shoulders and her mass of curls and large expressive eyes could easily steal a man's heart away. He mentally retreated. A man had to be careful, Maurice thought, hoping that it was not already too late.

That night set the pattern for Jenny's stay. Daytime saw her visiting shops, museums, galleries, and gardens. Most evenings she would enjoy a meal with Maurice in one of the numerous cafés and restaurants that he took such pleasure in introducing her to. She looked forward to them, yet at the same time became worried that he may expect more.

ת ת ת ת ת

One day, Jenny voiced her concerns to Judith, because she didn't want to lead him on.

"Maurice obviously finds you very attractive, Jenny," the other girl commented.

"I suspect he finds every woman attractive who's not over the age of ninety, and then it's a bit iffy," Jenny said with an amused smile.

"Seriously though," Judith laughed. "Don't you find him just a teeny bit appealing?"

"Of course I do," Jenny said. "He's just not my type of man, but I do like him as a friend."

"Honestly! Jenny, can't you just let go and have fun?" Judith folded her arms. "Enjoy his company while you're here?"

"Why can't I have fun without sleeping with him, because that's what you were implying, wasn't it?" Jenny put her hands on her hips, frowning at her friend impatiently. "If he doesn't mind, why should you?"

"I'm sorry, I know I should mind my own business, but I just hate to see you eating your heart out for some undeserving man," her friend said, apologetically.

Jenny felt upset by this reminder of something she had tried so hard to forget. "What makes you think that I'm pining for someone?" she questioned, trying to wrack her brains for anything in her demeanour which had exposed her innermost pain.

"Oh, Jenny, you are so transparent, at least you are to me. I told you, I've been through enough troubles of my own with men, so I know heartache when I see it, no matter how cleverly you might think that you've disguised it."

Jenny sank on to the nearest seat, feeling raw and exposed, and she realised that no matter how deeply she tried to bury her love for Darius, it would always be there. She despaired of a future that was blighted by the continuous presence in her head that she couldn't seem to erase, and yet Jenny must push him to the back of her mind and mentally slam the door on him. Surely, he would fade given time. Life had plenty to offer. Her work was selling well and now there was the added bonus of the 'Charrier' outlet. The stay in Paris had been an uplifting experience and she had, up until now, been having a wonderful time. Jenny had only a few days of her holiday left and she was determined to make the most of them.

ᛖᛖᛖᛖᛖᛖ

Darius, meanwhile, decided he had to get away from his family before they threw him out. He knew his behaviour was becoming less than acceptable and this was reinforced when Gina and Dominic cornered him and tore him off a strip. He sat and let their angry tirade wash over him, knowing that he richly deserved it, even seeing the humour in it. He, the elder brother, who had always lectured them about bad behaviour.

They were taken aback when Darius meekly agreed with their every word and promised to sort himself out. When they had left him, he sat and stared at the phone, wondering if Jonathan could bear to tolerate his company again. His life up until this year had been going well. It had been organised and calm. Darius had arranged his days methodically and any dinner dates were with girls who, like himself, wanted no commitments. Some, he had to admit, got ideas after they had been out with him a few times, but Darius had always been able to slide out of the situation with little trouble leaving good feelings on both sides. Although he was starting to worry a little about Melissa's constant presence.

Darius had never actually slept with her, but he was well aware that she would not be averse to the idea, and he didn't want to become too entangled with someone so domineering. Not that he was drawn to her anyway, and now with the constant image of Jenny in his troubled mind, he stood no chance of having a relationship with anybody, even a fleeting one. He cursed as a sudden longing coursed through him. This had to stop. He had no chance of a normal life until he had erased the memory of Jenny from his mind.

Darius finally plucked up his courage and called his friend. "Could you do with some company, Jonathan? I promise you that I'll try not to blight your life too much this time, but I just have to get away again."

He needn't have worried; his amiable friend was only too pleased to let him have the use of his villa. "Come over when you like, Darius, you know that you're welcome anytime," Jonathan said warmly. "So, your problems are not resolved, I take it? What you need is to relax in this calming sunshine and be alone. I'll be busy myself, as I have some business to attend to in Italy. You know where the key is. Let yourself in and make yourself at home. I'll be back in about two days, so I'll see you then."

Darius gratefully packed his bags and left on the first available flight, took a taxi from the airport, and arrived tired and dishevelled at his friend's door. He searched for the key and was surprised when the door opened, and he saw Jonathan standing smiling in welcome at him.

"My business appointment has been pushed back, so welcome, my friend, come in and put those heavy bags down."

Darius was relieved that Jonathan was there to greet him. His friend's good-natured manner was a balm to his spirits. Jonathan poured him a drink and placed it in his hand. "Here, get that down you, and sit and relax while I whip up a meal. You must be hungry."

"I haven't been eating well lately, and yet suddenly I feel ravenous." Darius nodded in surprise.

"It's the invigorating air here, nothing like it to perk up the old appetite," Jonathan grinned. "That and your journey, of course. You must be feeling a bit jaded."

Darius smiled back, glad of his friend's uncomplicated company. Jonathan always seemed to be so laid back. As a result, he found himself gradually unwinding and regaling his sympathetic friend with the problems that had beset him. That night, Darius slept better than he had for a very long time.

He spent most of his days just laying back in a lounger, totally tuning the world out, while his friend went off to attend the business meeting he had delayed. When Jonathan came back, he was concerned to observe the way his friend seemed to have no interest in what was going on around him. It was so unlike Darius. Obviously, it fell to him to try and jog Darius out of it, and he laid his plans accordingly.

"Darius, we need to liven you up a bit. Relaxing is one thing, letting your mind shut down is another. Come to Paris with me and become part of the living again."

Darius was resting back on a sun bed and turned his head lazily to face his friend. "I'm not particularly interested, thanks, Jonathan."

"Nonsense, you must snap out of this depression. As it happens, I've already arranged our stay in Paris at a nice quiet hotel. You'll like it."

He wandered off before Darius could make any protest and he sat up angrily. "Now look here, Jonathan," he called. "I don't feel like going out on the town, so you're wasting your time and even if I do come with you, I won't be any sort of company." By this time, he had stalked angrily after his friend and cornered him in the kitchen.

Jonathan was sitting at the breakfast bar, sipping coffee, and reading a newspaper. He looked up and saw the stubborn set expression on his friend's face. Ignoring the look, he informed Darius blandly that he had made a booking at one of the top restaurants with a business colleague and his wife.

"You'll like them both. Nice couple. The wife, Celeste, is a charming and amusing woman. He's only in town for a couple of days and expressed a desire to meet with you. I guess he's heard of your reputation, and this is a good business opportunity, Darius." Jonathan lifted his cup, looking innocently at his friend over the rim, knowing that he had Darius trapped. It would now look extremely rude of him not to appear.

"You are a very devious man," he snapped at Jonathan.

"I know," his friend grinned. "That's why I get on so well in the business world."

"Sorry, Jonathan, I have no right to inflict my bad humour on you." Darius gave a reluctant laugh, knowing when he was beaten. "Of course I'll come with you, and I promise to be on my best behaviour."

Darius was not to know that his friend had phoned Dominic the night before and had pumped him for information. Some of which James had provided, with Rachel's permission. Now Jonathan knew exactly where his friend's heart lay, and also where the lady in question was staying.

Chapter Sixteen

Jenny had two days left of her holiday and was feeling better than she had in a long time. This evening, Maurice was collecting her early and taking her to a show and then on to dinner. The non-stop whirl of theatres and dances had been wearing, but thoroughly enjoyable, and she would be sorry when it all ended. Yet it would be nice to get back to her quiet existence in the village and just drift along on that slower tide.

The evening came and Jenny chose a maroon velvet dress, which looked deceptively simple. It was beautifully cut, with a low neckline and long sleeves and on Jenny it looked fabulous.

Judith clapped her hands when she saw her friend standing in front of the mirror putting her earrings on.

"Oh, my word, Jenny, you look incredibly fantastic in that outfit. Don't be surprised if Maurice proposes tonight."

"Judith! You are joking, I hope?" Jenny whirled around, her face a mask of horror. "You don't really think he's taken all this seriously, do you?"

"No, no, it was just a figure of speech, a joke," Judith stammered, sorry to have upset Jenny in this way, "I can see that it was a stupid joke now. You know I say foolish things at times, just go and enjoy yourself."

By the time Maurice had come to collect her, Jenny had stopped worrying. Judith had done her best to reduce the fear she had instilled in her friend and assured her that Maurice never took life seriously. She just hoped that this was not the one time he had chosen to do so. Jenny was further reassured by Maurice's outrageous flirting, from the moment he collected her and up until he guided her into the restaurant, over to their table and helped her into a seat. He lifted his wine glass and looked at her warmly. "To our mutual friendship and future business dealings."

"I will drink to that willingly." She smiled at him, feeling her heart warm to this extremely likable man, as they touched glasses.

"Perhaps there could be more between us, who knows." He leaned forward, saying throatily. "What do you say, ma chérie?"

Jenny could tell by his open grin that he was not too serious, more an opportunist. She knew that he would like to get her into bed, and it was flattering. The fact that Jenny also knew that Maurice would like to bed half the women in France, made it less so, but for all that, he was a charming and attentive escort.

"Maurice, you are a very intelligent and attractive man, and I like you very much." Jenny reached across and patted his hand.

"Like!" He recoiled as though she had struck him. "Ah! 'Like', such an insipid word." Maurice looked so theatrically shocked, that she laughed.

"Oh, come on, you know you 'like' most of the women you meet. Besides, I value your friendship too much and taking it further might just spoil that."

He put his hand on his heart and looked mortally wounded, then his lips broke into a smile. "You like me a little, yes? It is a good start to our affair." Maurice threw his head back and laughed at her expression. Jenny was regarding him with a mixture of wariness and humour. "I tease you. You are so serious."

"I never quite know how to take you, Maurice," she sighed, with a faint laugh.

"Seriously, Jenny, could you not find it in your heart to make a little room for me?" He leaned forward again, covering her hand with his. Jenny gazed back at him with such sorrow before she lowered her eyes, that Maurice felt a surge of pity. "I am not he, am I?" he said gently.

"I beg your pardon?" Her startled eyes glanced back up at him.

"I am not this much desired man that you miss so very much," Maurice elaborated softly.

To her own horror, Jenny felt tears well up and sniffed as she fumbled for a tissue. She had thought that Darius had been successfully buried, that he no longer overshadowed all her days, and had subsided to a nagging ache. Now with a few words from Maurice, she had turned back into a pathetic, snivelling heap. A handkerchief was thrust into her hands and Jenny clutched it gratefully, blotting carefully at the tears before they spoilt her makeup.

"I am so sorry, Maurice, what a terrible thing to do to you, to spoil your meal like this."

"Nonsense, until this dramatic display, the evening was going well." Maurice gave her a charming smile. "I have enjoyed our time together. I forgive you for drenching my dinner table in tears."

"Oh! Maurice, you are such a nice man." Jenny laughed tremulously.

"Please! ...my reputation." He threw his hands up in mock horror. "To be called nice is, as you know, not something that I take kindly to." He smiled humorously at her, and she made an effort to get a grip on her emotions.

"Thank you, Maurice, for being so understanding." Jenny reached across and rested her hand on his, dabbing once more at her eyes to remove any remaining traces of tears, so she did not see the flash of emotion in his own eyes. When Jenny looked at him again, Maurice was once more in control of himself, and his open smiling face gazed back at her in commiseration.

"It has passed," he asked, "This momentary weakness for such an undeserving imbecile?"

Jenny found, to her own annoyance, that she wanted to defend Darius, and shook herself impatiently. "I'm fine, really, Maurice. Now let's pretend that I didn't just make an utter fool of myself and enjoy the rest of the evening."

Jenny glanced down at the menu, changing the subject, pointing to an item she could not understand and asking his advice. The meal was delicious, and Maurice soon charmed her into a lighter mood.

"You have been a good friend to me on this holiday, Maurice, thank you for showing me so many interesting places, and for sharing your company. I know that you're a very busy man." She smiled contentedly at him.

"I will give you a shoulder to cry on any time," he grinned back. Then added in a low sensuous voice. "Or better yet, a willing body to lay upon."

"Maurice, will you behave yourself," she laughed, in amusement, touching his hand lightly with her own.

It was at that moment that a man paused by their table and when he did not move away, Jenny glanced up curiously, only to wish she hadn't. Her heart seemed to lodge in her throat, as she was pierced by cold glittering black eyes.

"Enjoying yourself?" Darius said, through clenched teeth, as he switched his gaze to size up her companion. "What are you doing here, of all places?"

He turned his eyes back to Jenny, as he waited impatiently for a reply and it was obvious from his rigid body that Darius was not going to leave until she gave him an answer, but Jenny was bereft of words and could only continue to stare silently up at him. Maurice sat and observed with curiosity, this large man who was the cause of such misery in his little friend. He did not look so happy himself, and Maurice could only wonder what it was that prevented the two from getting together. His own world was not so tiresomely complicated, and he could not understand their problem.

"Dance with me," Darius said abruptly.

Jenny looked up at him uncomprehendingly, only now becoming aware of the people that had taken to the floor in the centre of the restaurant and were dancing to soft music. "I'm sorry," she stammered. "As you can see, I have company."

"I'm sure that your friend would not mind," Darius said curtly, tearing his eyes away from her for a brief second, to gaze down at Maurice with stony eyes. "We have your permission?"

"Please, do not be concerned on my account," Maurice smiled amiably and spread his hands. "Go, dance with your friend, and enjoy the music. You will, of course, come back to me at the end." A statement that had Darius giving him a challenging look, which Maurice blandly ignored with a mocking smile on his face.

Darius moved Jenny's chair out as she stood up, and as the room was crowded, she had to brush closely against him while manoeuvring around the chair. He sucked his breath in as they touched. It seemed that she still had the same potent effect on him as ever.

Jenny shivered as Darius pulled her body hard against his on the crowded dance floor, but her attempt to put some distance between them was thwarted by the close proximity of other people. His hand on her back was caressing and forcing her closer still, and she could feel the hot breath from the lips that hovered dangerously near to her cheek. Her own body betrayed her, instantly responding to the hard muscled torso pressed so closely against her. Jenny only had to turn her head a fraction to unleash something she was in no condition to handle.

"Who is he?" Darius demanded curtly, his face grim.

"A friend, a very good one," she emphasised with a frown.

"More than a friend?" he probed angrily.

"None of your business," Jenny said heatedly. "I don't quiz you about your special women friends, do I?"

"Special women friends," Darius echoed sharply. "What is that supposed to mean?"

Jenny evaded his penetrating gaze. She did not particularly want to open that personal wound and felt vulnerable and fragile. She did not feel up to verbally sparring with this man so disturbingly close now. Jenny just wanted to escape. "Let me go, Darius," she said, pushing frantically against his arms. He couldn't hold on to her without causing a scene, so he reluctantly let her pull away.

Jenny did not hear his anguished. "I only wish I could," as she fled back to her table. Maurice glanced from her distressed face to the towering, equally miserable, distraught man gazing longingly after her, and decided that now might be a good time to make their departure.

י ני ני ני ני ני

Jonathan and his friends were waiting for Darius to get back to their table. The colleague, because he wanted to discuss a business proposition with him, and Jonathan, because he had watched with an open mouth as Darius stopped talking in the middle of a sentence. His gaze had fixed like a hawk onto a table at the other side of the room and Darius had nearly tipped his chair over in his haste to go over and accost the couple sitting there, who were obviously enjoying each other's company. He had also observed the interaction between the two on the dance floor. Jonathan's mouth quirked, that must be the shortest dance on record and yet one could see the obvious sexual tension between them. It had drawn more than one set of eyes, so what the hell was the problem?

When they arrived back at their hotel room, Darius threw himself into the nearest chair like a petulant child. Although he was annoyed by his own behaviour, his anger at this moment was directed toward his friend. He frowned accusingly up at Jonathan. "Now tell me that little meeting was a complete coincidence!"

Jonathan leaned back comfortably on the bed, regarding his friend with raised brows "And if it were not?" he drawled.

"I will kill you for interfering, and as you can see, it didn't do an atom of good. Quite the reverse," Darius snarled.

"Rubbish! It was probably your lack of charm that rubbed her up the wrong way. I bet you said something you shouldn't have." Jonathan smiled, to soften his words. "Why don't you go and pay her a visit, clear all this up. It just so happens that I know where she's staying."

"I thought you might." Darius stared at him, humour vying with anger. Then he shrugged resignedly. "Anyway, I stand no chance. Jenny was with another man."

"So, she was with another man, which doesn't mean there was anything going on. It didn't stop you asking her to dance, and he seemed to have no objection to you whisking her off," his friend said impatiently. Then he added in a goading voice. "What are you, a man, or a mouse?"

Darius stood up, his fists clenching with impotent anger and took a step towards him, one large fist actually rising.

"Whoa! Hang on there." Jonathan held his hands up in mock fear. "Remember, I am much smaller than you."

Darius found himself subsiding and giving a grudging laugh, as he dropped his hands. "Don't be such a bloody fool, Jonathan," he said, shaking his head. "You know darn well that I wouldn't really have hit you, and besides, you're only a couple of inches shorter than me."

"An inch, if you don't mind," Jonathan protested, indignantly. They both laughed at this reference to an old bone of contention between them.

Chapter Seventeen

Darius brooded about his friend's suggestion and then decided to give it one last try. He would go and see Jenny. He knew that it was getting late, but he desperately needed this chance to speak with her.

When the knock came at the door, Jenny smiled and shook her head. Surely Judith had not forgotten her key yet again, it had become quite a habit of late. She opened the door with a smile on her face, which rapidly disappeared as Jenny saw who was standing there.

Darius's large hand stopped her from closing the door on him, and she was pushed backwards, as his broad shoulders moved the door effortlessly aside. He stood in front of her, hands hanging loosely at his sides, and gazed down with an intensity that made Jenny swallow nervously.

"What do you want, Darius?" she whispered.

"You know the answer to that," he replied harshly, putting his hands in his pockets as though to confine them, and stop them reaching out for her. He cleared his throat, moving restlessly from one foot to another. "How are you?" he asked abruptly.

Jenny tried to answer, but no sound emerged, so she swallowed and tried again. "I am very well, thank you," she replied stiltedly. Why was he here? Apart from peeling away her carefully built-up layers of armour, he didn't seem to know what to say, and his manner was now distant and cold. Then she ventured a glance up into the dark eyes that were fixed so intently upon her and Jenny saw that she had been mistaken in thinking his manner detached. The hot desire that gleamed back at her, made her heartbeat accelerate wildly. She felt as though her feet were anchored to the floor as Darius groaned and reached for her, and moaned helplessly as their mouths met with an explosive force that jerked her head back, making her legs buckle weakly as his urgent body moved against hers in time to his probing tongue.

His muttered, incoherent words were not heard by the mindless girl in his arms, and then speech deserted Darius entirely as, in feverish haste, he moved her backwards into the bedroom. He lifted his head to draw in a gasping breath and then froze as his eyes caught sight of a man's pyjamas protruding from beneath the pillow.

Jenny felt his body go rigid and draw away. She looked up in confusion and felt shocked by the withdrawn and harshly set look to his white face, wondering what had caused the sudden change in his manner.

"Are you staying here alone?" Darius asked, his eyes narrowed and watchful.

"No," Jenny said slowly, as she followed the cold gaze he directed at the bed, and her throat closed with unshed tears as she saw the suspicion on his face. "I'm staying with a friend." Jenny remained silent, as she waited to see his reaction to this statement and Darius rapidly put some distance between them, as though he could not bear to touch her.

"Why did you let me make such a fool of myself!" he raged.

"You don't need my help to do that," she snapped, hurt beyond belief as she realised what he was thinking. Jenny felt a slow anger burning in her that overrode her bitter sorrow and glared up at him. "I think this would be a good time for you to leave." She slipped around him and marched to the front door, holding it open, standing quietly waiting for him to go.

"If you are so enamoured of your 'friend', why did you let me kiss you and why are you protecting him?" Darius stalked past her, stopped in the doorway, and added nastily. "I can guess who it is."

"I did not *let* you kiss me; you caught me off guard, that's all, and I would fiercely defend anyone from someone like you," Jenny shouted.

"Someone like me?" he repeated slowly, through tight lips.

"Yes, so condemning of other people, jumping to conclusions. All the wrong ones, of course," she added scornfully.

Darius knew instantly without her telling him that he had made a ghastly mistake and wanted to speak to her again, make a fresh start, but he could see by the cold, shuttered hurt on Jenny's face that at this moment it would be a complete waste of time. He felt his heart sink. Once again, his own insane jealousy had put another brick in the wall that he was rapidly building between them. He gazed at her, his dark eyes troubled, not knowing how to penetrate that icy shell.

"I'm sorry," Darius said quietly, as he turned and walked out. He could still hear the ill-chosen words that had emerged from his mouth. He went over them again and again as she slammed the door behind him with enough force to shatter his eardrums, and Darius felt worse by the minute.

When Darius turned up at his hotel room, he looked to be in a worse state than when he had left, and Jonathan threw his hands up in despair.

"What happened this time?" He put his hands out, palms up. "No! Don't tell me, let me guess. You made some stupid, insanely jealous remark."

Darius stared at him, his shoulders hunched in an attitude of abject despair, his eyes dark with misery, too dejected even to retaliate. Then he walked silently away into his bedroom and shut the door quietly behind him.

Jonathan stared at the closed door helplessly. So much for well-laid plans, he thought in exasperation.

Darius stayed with his friend for two more days, talking himself into a more positive frame of mind and when he was packing his case to leave, he felt that he had finally achieved a measure of normality. Once more Jonathan watched with a concerned face as his friend packed. He was not fooled by the veneer of apparent control. He had weathered that same stormy sea himself, and Jonathan knew that Darius was hurting badly.

As they parted company and Darius climbed into the taxi that came to collect him for his trip to the airport, Jonathan could see the almost draining effort his friend was making to try and look relaxed.

"There goes an extremely tormented man," he muttered with heartfelt sympathy as Jonathan watched the car whisk his friend away, back to the same old problems. There was no other way of helping him, much as Jonathan would like to, but at least he had left Darius with a standing invitation to stay whenever things got on top of him again.

꒜꒜꒜꒜꒜꒜

Jenny was also hurting, her wounds not as deeply buried as she had hoped. She had already left Paris and was winging her way homewards, the holiday completely spoilt. It appalled her to think that she had nearly given in to Darius again, in fact would have done so like a silly, weak lovesick fool if he had not stopped when he did. She berated herself all the way home, wanting to collapse with grief, yet having to hold it all back, because Judith, who also had to get back to her job, was travelling with her. No amount of commiseration or words of wisdom from her friend provided any comfort for her bruised heart, and Jenny was looking forward to the privacy of her own bedroom to give way to her hard held tears.

Maurice had seen them off and the kind concern on his face had nearly been the undoing of Jenny's carefully constructed cocoon. She had hugged him gratefully, then waved farewell with real regret. If it had not been for Darius filling her heart and mind, she might just have fallen for him.

Maurice stood looking at the gate they had disappeared through, long after they had gone. "Ah!" he sighed. "There goes a tiny piece of my soul, I fear." Then he caught the eye of an attractive woman, who gave him a coquettish smile as she passed, and Maurice brightened. All was well in his world.

Chapter Eighteen

Darius was deep in his own unhappy thoughts and didn't hear his father's question until it was repeated in a controlled roar. "For the third and last time, Darius, what is all this about an engagement?"

"Engagement?" Darius looked at his father blankly. "Whose engagement?"

"Yours, of course! I was reliably informed by Melissa's father at the golf club that your engagement was imminent. You can understand my chagrin when I had to admit to him that I knew nothing at all about it. Shouldn't we have been informed of such an important event?"

"I would have done had I any intention of becoming engaged! I am not, nor ever will be engaged to Melissa. There is only one person who wished for that." Darius sat up straight, his body rigid with anger and turned his eyes accusingly to Isabel. "Now where could she possibly have gained such a preposterous idea from?"

"Melissa must have overheard me," Isabel, blurted nervously, conscious of all the watching eyes on her.

"Go on," Charles drawled, his brows lowering, as his eyes fixed on hers. "Do tell us, Isabel, who were you telling of this momentous occasion?"

Isabel was horrified by her own thoughtless words which had virtually condemned her. Why couldn't she have just denied all knowledge of the story? Just silly gossip she could have said. Now she was at a loss to explain her actions. Too late for lies, and nobody else to blame. She cleared her suddenly dry throat, as she felt hot colour surge up into her face. "That girl."

"What girl?" Darius asked in a tight angry voice, his suspicions aroused.

"The one in the shop," Isabel whispered, swallowing anxiously at his thunderous expression.

"And what were your exact words?" Charles said almost gently.

"I told her Darius was getting engaged to Melissa and invited her to the party." Her voice died in a reedy whisper, as both men fixed her with stony eyes.

"No wonder Jenny wouldn't have anything to do with me," Darius groaned, as he slumped back tiredly in his seat. He was not to know that Melissa had made the whole situation far worse.

"I didn't realise that you thought so much of her. I thought it was just a casual fling, that she might be pursuing you." Isabel at least refrained from adding that she thought the girl unsuitable and began to feel guilty at the outcome of her interference. Her composure started to crack as her stepson glanced up with fierce anger.

"How could you do such a spiteful thing? No wonder Jenny hates me. I love her..." His voice broke on the words, and Darius jumped up, leaving the room before he did something he might regret.

Isabel felt terrible and her heartbeat accelerated in growing fear as she observed the accusing faces regarding her. She was a selfish, often childlike woman and in her own eyes seldom did anything wrong. Now Isabel knew without a doubt that she had interfered once too often. She gave a start of surprise as her husband came rapidly around the table, grabbed her shoulders, and shook her.

"You are an interfering, overbearing, selfish, stupid woman," he raged, then suddenly let go as though he could not bear to touch her. Charles had never been this violent with her before and it shocked her.

They were all taken aback by his actions, even more so when her set white face unexpectedly crumpled, and Isabel began to heave with body racking sobs that tore at her, stealing her breath away, causing her to stumble in an ungainly manner as she made for the nearest chair. She sat with her hands pressed to her face, trying to gain control of herself. She felt like hiding, but there was no escaping this situation, and that it was of her own making just made the whole thing worse. Her broken words were hard to decipher as she first began to speak. Then Isabel made an effort and spoke more clearly.

"I'm sorry, I am so very sorry," she sobbed. "I know that you all hate me, and I can't take it anymore." The tears rolled steadily down her face as she spoke, and they all stared at her in embarrassed silence, finding it hard to believe that this slumped figure was the hard, always composed Isabel. "You will be pleased to know that I shall now arrange to go away as soon as possible. I can see that you will all be better off without me." She looked up through swimming eyes, giving a laughing sob as she caught the look that passed between them. "Oh! Don't worry, I won't inflict myself on you again" Isabel gulped, and her voice broke on the words, and it took some while for her to gain control and speak again.

She leaned back and dropped her hands to her lap, then gazed sadly at their father. "I give up, Charles. I am so terribly sorry to have embarrassed you in front of the children. You may find it amusing to know that I still love you, but you've never really wanted me here, so I'll make it easy for you and take my leave." Isabel's voice faltered and her mouth clamped into a tight line, as her emotions threatened to overcome her again. She gave a small grimace. "I know that I can be silly, even childish at times and I expect a psychiatrist would have a field day if they were to try and analyse me. They would probably say that it was a bid for attention on my part and perhaps they would be right. I know that I've handled everything badly from the very start of our relationship, Charles, and I apologise once again. It's quite obvious that I never fitted in here, nor ever will."

Charles was staring down at the dishevelled Isabel as though he had never seen her before. That apology was quite something, coming as it did from his wife. Isabel made as if to rise, but Charles hunkered down in front of her forlorn figure, gathering her shaking body into his arms and began murmuring quiet words of comfort that only she could hear.

Gina signalled to the others to follow her from the room, and they silently obeyed. Each of them in varying degrees felt pity for Isabel. They could not love her, but perhaps if she was genuinely contrite and made an effort to change, maybe in time they would come to at least, if not like, respect her.

Gina stood listening to the lowered voices from behind the closed door and wondered about Isabel. She still felt shocked by the other woman's unexpected display of emotion. They say leopards don't change their spots, she mused, and Isabel could be devious to get her own way.

If this was a change of tactics, it was certainly working. Yet she had never seen the older woman break down or ever admit that she was wrong before. Somehow Gina felt that this was the real Isabel, and she could get to quite like this different version.

She felt slightly guilty, because to be fair to Isabel, it had been an uphill struggle for the poor woman with three children to suddenly cope with and expecting twins herself. None of the children had made her task any easier with their resentment at this glamorous replacement for their mother. Had she been more capable of a patient love, eventually Isabel might have won them over. Her own immaturity had contributed to her inability to cope with the situation, and she had handled it with her usual lack of finesse. Her father's reaction had also surprised her. Gina had thought all love extinguished between the two, but the spark was obviously still there, judging by the compassionate look on his face as he held his wife.

Charles smoothed Isabel's hair away from her wet and swollen eyes and pressed a kiss to her brow. She looked like a clown, mascara smeared her cheeks and her lipstick was smudged, yet he felt his heart beat a little faster and a love that he had long thought dormant stirred within him. He gave her his large handkerchief and helped her to repair the ravages her crying bout had inflicted.

Isabel stared at him, suddenly feeling shy at this gentle and caring Charles. She gave him a tentative smile. "Did you mean what you said. Charles? Do you still love me a little and want me to stay?"

He gazed at her tenderly. He rather liked this vulnerable woman who clung so desperately to his arms. "Of course I meant it, my darling. You know me, never say anything I don't mean."

Isabel suppressed a sob of gratitude and clung more tightly, her arms sliding around his neck.

"I can't face the others yet. Can't we go away from here," she begged.

"Good idea, and it had already crossed my mind, as it happens," Charles smiled slowly at her, his old familiar loving smile that Isabel had thought never to see again, and more tears filled her eyes. "Hey! Come on. Don't go all watery on me again," he whispered, holding her securely against him.

Isabel clung to him like a lifeline, frightened to let go. Let this not be a dream, let him love me like he used to, Isabel thought desperately. She would take whatever he cared to show her, as long as he forgave her.

Charles felt her fear and tension and held her close. They sat like that for a long time, until the light began to fade, making plans together.

ロ ロ ロ ロ ロ ロ

Gina hated to see her brother so depressed and persuaded him that it might be best if he went right away again, if only to keep away from Isabel. In the mood he was in, if they met there could be another very unpleasant scene, and one had been quite enough for the present. She didn't tell him that their father and stepmother were already planning their own departure. Darius needed time away from all of them to sort himself out, and Rachel constantly turning up with James would not help the situation if he stayed.

Darius had decided to do what Gina recommended. In his present mood he would be next to useless at work and could easily delegate. Any one of his brothers was just as capable as he was of handling the business while he was away. His colleagues would probably hold a party and put banners out to celebrate his departure, after the foul mood he had been in lately. He had put a damper on everything and everybody.

Darius stood disconsolately, hands in pockets, watching as his sister took over his packing. "I can pack my own bag, you know. Stop nannying me," he said quietly.

Gina ignored him and went on packing methodically. "I like packing for you. Where have you decided to go?"

"I thought Devon might be nice. Quiet, you know." He avoided her eyes as she glanced around.

Gina turned back to the bag, so he did not see the knowing smile that curved her lips. Her brother was so transparent. "Any particular place in Devon?" she inquired, innocently.

"No," he said. "Nowhere special."

He was so quiet that Gina turned around again, and Darius flushed as he realised that she could see right through him.

"Is that wise, Darius, to go there of all places?" He looked so miserable that she wanted to hold him close to her. "Oh! Darius."

"Don't worry about me, Gina. I'm old enough to cope with my own problems. Going there will help me to come to terms with all this." He closed his eyes and rubbed a weary hand over his face. He tried to laugh, but it emerged as a harsh sigh. "I viewed myself as fairly mature before this all happened, but rejection is harder to handle than I would have thought."

Gina's heart bled for him. He was always so strong, and to see him like this was unbearable. She put her arms around him and gave him a fierce hug. "Go if you feel you must and at least try to relax. Things may turn out better than you think."

If Darius had been his normal alert self, he may have taken heed of her words.

Chapter Nineteen

Gradually Jenny built a protective shell around herself, and was coping quite well, or so she thought. The ring at the door made her jump and for one forlorn moment she thought it might be Darius. It was a silly hope, why would he ever want to see her, when Jenny had made it so clear that she didn't want him to contact her ever again.

When she opened the door and saw who her visitor was, her eyes filled with tears. "Oh! Gina, come in, although I can't imagine what we have to talk about."

"I didn't know that I made such a terrible impression on people." Gina raised her eyebrows. She indicated Jenny's tear-filled eyes and said "Does it not occur to you that if James and Rachel get married, we would be nearly related? We would be almost like sisters-in-law, so you will have to get used to me. Surely my company isn't too awful to contemplate?"

Jenny blushed at her own bad manners, she liked Gina and would hate to think that she had hurt her in any way. "Sorry, Gina, that was thoughtless of me. You know that I value your friendship." The tears spilled over. "It's just that I had started to sort myself out and seeing you has resurrected it all again. You know, of course, that I love him." Her voice ended in a wail, as Jenny finished speaking and she sank down into a chair, letting her tears flow freely.

"Jenny, will you listen to me? Just let me talk." Gina looked down at the hunched figure with compassion. "Please try and understand. Darius did not trust to give his love to any woman. Commitment is something he has always shied away from. Did you know that he was with mother when she died, and he was only thirteen years old, and Dominic eleven. Darius wouldn't leave her side when she became ill and I was only about four myself, so I didn't quite know what was really happening, but he, being the elder, felt it terribly."

"Oh! poor Darius," Jenny cried in distress, as she lifted her tearstained face.

"You have a soft heart, Jenny," Gina smiled. "Perhaps it will help to make you understand how Darius's mind works. He loved our mother desperately and she left him. He wanted to love Isabel, and he felt rejected by her, because unfortunately she did not see him as a child, only an extremely attractive young man. He was fifteen when father remarried and very tall for his age."

"You mean she made a play for him?" Jenny's eyes widened.

"Oh! Nothing that bad, she loved my father too much for that." Gina saw the look of surprise that Jenny gave her. "Oh, yes, Isabel did love him madly at one time. Even as young as I was, I could see that. She just couldn't be a mother to Darius, it was too much for her vanity. She wanted his admiration, not a childish love. Of course, he felt lonely and hurt, as we all did, but Darius felt it the most. Unfortunately, all his girlfriends have had a tendency to be from the same mould; glamorous, but not serious. I think he has kept it that way deliberately, to prevent getting hurt again."

"Why are you telling me all this? What difference does it make to me to hear about his avoidance of commitment, apart from telling me what I already know, and what of his engagement?" Jenny stared up at her.

"How much convincing do you need? Get this straight, Jenny, once and for all. There is no engagement, no marriage on the horizon, unless it's between you and Darius. That was all in Isabel's mind, and wishful thinking on Melissa's part, so for heaven's sake put him out of his misery. I can't bear to see him suffer like this; he loves you desperately, Jenny." Gina frowned down at her. She put her hand up as Jenny went to protest and paused waiting to see what effect her words would have on the dejected figure in front of her. When Jenny still made no reply, she sank down beside her on the couch and gazed earnestly at her. "I mean it, he really is deeply in love with you. Darius is just afraid to tell you in case he gets knocked back. I have never seen him like this. Never. He needs to know that you love him, Jenny, no strings."

"No strings," repeated Jenny slowly. She twisted her lips. "I could get badly hurt that way." Gina could not know how much she had already suffered at her brother's hands, and Jenny wasn't sure if she could live through such agony again.

Jenny sat where Gina had left her, going over the information that her friend had given her. Her mind went back to Darius and her last encounter with him. She remembered his words and the way he had looked. He had been genuinely concerned for her and totally dejected. Just before he had turned to leave, she had glimpsed something in his eyes, a lost hopeless look and something else. Jenny sat and thought about that look for a very long time. She felt a dawning wonderment and her spirits soared. Not just lust then.

ℶ ℶ ℶ ℶ ℶ ℶ

Jenny set about her plans with renewed energy, a few important phone calls and she was ready.

When Rachel had finished in the shop and entered the flat, she found her sister in a strange and excited mood. Cases were open on the bed and clothes were strewn about haphazardly. This was not a bit like Jenny.

"What's going on here?" Rachel asked worriedly, as she stared at her sisters flushed face.

"I am going away," Jenny announced.

"I can see that. Where are you going?" Rachel inquired.

"I just need to get away," her sister stated defensively. "At least you'll be without my miserable face for a while."

"You don't look particularly miserable to me." Rachel studied her sister, with her head tilted thoughtfully. "What happened to make you snap out of your depression?"

"Darius happened." Jenny glanced up at her, as she continued sorting her clothes out.

"I thought he was the lowest of the low, the ultimate bottomless pit of slime." Rachel said, in disbelief. "A cesspool of sludge, to use your own words."

"He was and is, but he loves me." Jenny laughed in amusement at the startled look on her sister's face. "He just hasn't admitted it yet."

"Oh! Jen, don't leave yourself wide open to hurt again." Rachel looked at her with deepening concern.

"I won't, I promise you." Jenny shook her head to reassure her, and carried on packing, not to be deterred. "All I want to do is to give him the chance to say the words if he can. If he doesn't, then he will be none the wiser as to my true feelings, and we can both move on with our lives."

"Are you sure this is such a good idea, Jen?" Rachel hovered anxiously as she continued packing.

Jenny's face was serious, and she stopped what she was doing and smiled. She looked into her sister's worried eyes and gave her a hug. "Don't fret about me, Rachel, I can't be hurt any more than I already have been." She returned to her task. "I won't do anything to cause myself pain or embarrassment."

Jenny would not have used the last word if she could have foreseen what lay ahead.

ഇ ഇ ഇ ഇ ഇ ഇ

Jenny sat looking out of the train window watching the scenery crawl by. She was eager to reach her destination and also petrified. She let her mind wander over Darius's face and closed her eyes, resting her head back against the seat. Jenny found her mind exploring his body as well and a hot tide of colour surged into her face, causing a faint groan to escape from her lips, which brought a strange look from the old lady opposite her. Jenny coughed and sat up, thumping her chest, and smiling apologetically at the woman. Then meekly took the cough sweet the woman so kindly offered her, and from then on was forced to make conversation with the talkative woman until, to her guilty relief, the elderly lady alighted at one of the small stations along the way.

She shifted impatiently on her seat. What was wrong with this darned train, why was it going so slow? Another leaf dropped on the line causing a jam, or a flake of snow? Then Jenny decided that she was glad it wasn't travelling faster, because she was having second thoughts about her decision to take this risky step. Suppose Darius was shocked and appalled to see her? Even worse, what if he was with another woman? Don't be silly, she scolded herself. Gina had assured her that he had gone away on his own and she had also insisted that Darius finally confessed that he loved her. Well, Jenny would soon find out, one way or another.

She caught a taxi from the station and felt her heart beating with fearful anticipation as she neared her destination. The taxi pulled up outside the pretty hotel, and Jenny climbed out slowly, gazing up at the beautiful old building appreciatively. She was sad to see that the old creeper was losing its leaves and wondered if this was a bad omen. An impatient cough reminded her to pay the cab driver, and the vehicle drove off leaving Jenny to face her fate. She had deliberately timed her arrival to coincide with the evening meal, because she was more likely to slip in unnoticed at this hour, as most people would be in the dining area eating. She was tired, nervous, and needed to sleep before she tackled Darius.

Jenny signed her name, casting her eyes quickly over the two pages facing her as the desk clerk turned to get her key, and saw Darius's name scrawled in a strong hand at the top. She glanced furtively around to make sure Darius was nowhere about, and much to her embarrassment, encountered a familiar face.

The manager smiled in recognition as he came over to her, and Jenny flushed as she wondered which part of her he was remembering.

"Hello, there, Miss Stayner, isn't it? I never forget a pretty face." He bit back a laugh as he realised that the girl was blushing. Better to pretend he had forgotten his last view of her. Not that he could, the manager thought with amusement. "Enjoy your stay. I will get your cases sent up shortly. Would you like a small tray of supper sent up?"

Jenny was suddenly aware, to her surprise, that she was quite hungry and accepted his kind suggestion. Then she made her way quickly up to her room. She put her things down on the bed and slowly sank onto a comfortable chair near the window. What was she letting herself in for, she wondered with a sense of dread, more heartache? Why had she let Gina persuade her that this was a good idea? She must want to have her head examined. Talk about asking for punishment. Never mind about that, she told herself sternly. This is something you have to tackle, so stop whingeing, and get on with it.

The knock at the door startled her, then she remembered her supper tray, and opening the door, took it gratefully. As she sat eating her meal, Jenny ran over various scenarios in her mind on how to approach Darius and discarded most of them. Her thoughts were becoming muddled with tired confusion, so she decided to try planning anew when she was fresh and alert in the morning.

That night, strangely enough and much to her own surprise, Jenny slept like the proverbial log. She woke up refreshed and ready to tackle whatever the day might bring.

Chapter Twenty

When Jenny went down to breakfast, there was no sign of Darius anywhere, nor was there for the rest of the day and Jenny began to worry. Surely, he had not left already. Another day passed, and still he had not made an appearance. Now she started to feel desperate. By lunchtime, she was becoming agitated and upset, then suddenly there he was. She was caught by surprise as Darius entered the room and hastily shrank back into her chair.

Jenny had placed herself strategically, slightly to one side of a large pot plant on a stand, and from where he stood Darius could not see her. Her heart surged with pity as she regarded him. He looked so tired and pale. His face looked drawn and his eyes empty, and Jenny wondered if that was on her behalf. She selfishly hoped it was.

Darius was ushered to a table by the manager, who leaned over him deferentially as he gave him the menu and Jenny stared at the man with an amused smile as he continued to fuss with the table setting. Yes, she thought, I suppose Darius does have that effect on people. She glanced around and saw several women regarding this tall, darkly handsome man, with more than just a passing interest. One even stopped at his table, smiling flirtatiously down at him as she spoke. Jenny found herself holding her breath as she waited to see his reaction to this invitation, then let it out in a rush as the woman's smile died and she flounced away. Jenny gave a small nervous laugh, as she wondered what his put-down had been, something caustic no doubt.

Darius's head whipped around, as though he had heard the faint laugh and recognised it. Jenny leaned back, frantically trying to bury herself in the fronds of the plant, but her efforts proved to be useless as her vision was suddenly filled by a large masculine body. Her head shot up and she stared mesmerised into his glittering black eyes.

"I thought it was you," Darius gritted. "What the hell are you doing here, come to haunt me have you, to gloat over me, to see how much...?" His voice tailed off as Darius realised what he had been about to give away.

Jenny closed her mouth and gazed up at him searchingly. His large hands were gripping the back of the chair beside her so tightly that she thought he might do it some damage. Confidence surged through her as she saw the emotion on his face, and in the way that Darius held himself so rigidly. Jenny grinned up at him impishly, a small dimple appearing in her cheek.

"I thought that I would take a nice, restful holiday. Recapture fond memories, so to speak."

Darius gazed at the dimple and then his look lingered on her soft lips.

Jenny drew her breath in as she saw his gaze darken with desire and she tried to control the thrill that coursed through her. At least he still wanted her, that surely was a hopeful sign. She schooled her face into a semblance of normality. "What shall we have for lunch?" she inquired brightly, opening the menu and pretending an interest.

"Pardon?" he said slowly and his eyes wavered, as though breaking out of a trance. Jenny repeated the question, and he sank down into the chair opposite.

"I've already ordered, but we might as well be sociable and eat together," Darius mumbled colourlessly.

As they ate, he was quiet and introspective, but his mood brightened as Darius observed her flushed cheeks and downcast eyes, the slight giveaway tremble in her hands. She gave him a quick glance and lowered her eyes again immediately, making a pretence of eating the food in front of her. Hope and confidence began to fill Darius, as he saw her barely controlled agitation. Then he asked himself the question, which should have occurred to him the moment he saw her. Why was she even here, if not to see him? He brightened up at the thought. "Enjoying your meal?" he queried softly.

They both looked down at the mashed jumble of food on her plate. "We have to talk Darius," Jenny said as she stared across at him.

"Yes, we do, don't we," he said in a low sensual voice that made goosebumps chase up and down her spine.

"I'm serious," Jenny said quietly.

"So am I." He reached across, took her hand, and pressed a warm kiss into her palm, sending another delicious shiver through her.

"Will you stop that and listen to me?" she breathed, closing her eyes briefly.

Darius was filled with elation at the look he had glimpsed, and a slow devilish smile formed on his face. "How about coming upstairs with me and making long, lingering love?" he said, softly. His smile shrivelled rapidly, and he began to doubt his own sanity, as her eyes widened, and she jerked back in her seat. What had possessed him to make such a stupid and presumptuous statement? Although, to his shame, he had to admit that he had half hoped she would take him up on the suggestion.

"How dare you!" Jenny squeaked, staring at him with her mouth open. Well, he certainly did not believe in wasting time. His words went down like a stone in a pool, leaving disturbing ripples. Yes, she would love to take him up on the offer, but shouldn't they at least talk first? The room went still as interested eyes swivelled their way. "Did you think I came here just to jump into bed with you?" she demanded angrily, not bothering to lower her voice.

"Well, didn't you?" Darius growled, equally as loudly, his own anger matching hers, although his was driven by rising guilt.

A faint gasp echoed around the small dining area, but they were oblivious, as they sat glaring at each other. Jenny jumped to her feet, snatched her jacket up, swung it around her shoulders and made to flounce out looking suitably insulted. Jenny just hoped he followed her.

Unfortunately, the edge of the material snagged on the plant pot, and Darius watched in resigned fascination as it descended from the shelf towards his head. He jerked away and the pot missed him by inches, then he went down in a heap as his chair, unbalanced by his sudden movement, toppled backwards. The witch, it seemed, was back with a vengeance. As Jenny fled, she heard one of the women say in a stage whisper. "Serves him right, I'd have brained him with the pot, as well." A titter rippled around the room and Jenny put her fingers to her mouth to quell the hysterical laughter that was bubbling beneath the surface.

Reaching her room, she slammed her door shut, leaned back, and closed her eyes. Could anything else possibly go wrong? she asked herself. So much for getting him in the right mood.

The door vibrated against her body as a large fist hit it.

"Let me in so that I can kill you slowly. It's only fair," Darius demanded. She stayed silent, then a lowered voice said petulantly. "It's my turn to harm you."

Jenny laughed helplessly and moved away from the door as it opened, and Darius peered round it cautiously. "Am I safe or are you going to attack me with something else?"

Jenny shook her head, suddenly feeling shy, and the way he was looking at her took her breath away causing her heart to thud erratically in her breast. "What are you doing?" she said shakily as he moved menacingly towards her.

Darius suddenly lunged for Jenny and pushed her backwards towards the bed. The breath was forced from her body as they landed together onto the mattress. "If I've got you in this position, nothing can happen to me... Right?" he said, pinning her down with his body. Jenny gulped and looked up into his laughing eyes, two inches above hers. "Lost for words at last?" he queried. He lowered his head as she opened her mouth to retaliate and his lips covered hers, his arms tightening around her, and Jenny was lost. She only surfaced when she felt the cool air on her skin.

"How did you get me undressed that quickly?" Jenny whispered.

"Practice," he answered huskily.

She shut her mind to the implications of that. What was past had nothing to do with here and now, and her mind was disintegrating as fast as her will power as his hands and mouth explored and manipulated her into giving in completely to his demands.

𒊹 𒊹 𒊹 𒊹 𒊹 𒊹

Jenny woke and tried to stretch her cramped limbs, but found her movements severely restricted by the large muscular body clamped firmly around hers. She tried a tentative push, but it was like trying to move a brick wall, and just waking Darius seemed to remind him that he had duties to perform, and he appeared to be making up for lost time. He could not get enough of her and Jenny had a job to eventually prise herself away from him.

"We have to stop for food, apart from anything else," she breathed against his mouth.

"Why?" he inquired, holding her tightly. "If I let you go, will you promise not to run away?" He laughed, but she could feel the tension in his body.

"Oh, I'll be back. Try and keep me away," Jenny whispered, as she eased herself apart from him.

They ordered a meal to be sent up and Jenny laughed as she sat watching Darius eat. "It's no use devouring it fast," she reprimanded him. "I like to take my time."

"So do I," he said huskily, pushing his chair back. She never did get to finish her own meal.

𒊹 𒊹 𒊹 𒊹 𒊹 𒊹

It was two days before they made another appearance in the dining room. Some of the women looked envious and smiled at the obvious love between these two good-looking people. Jenny gazed across at Darius as they ate their evening meal. He could hardly keep his hands off her, a fact that she was smugly aware of. She knew exactly how he felt because she was experiencing the same problem. His smouldering glances were also putting her off her food and she put her fork down. Her desire was tempered by anxiety. How exactly did she stand with him and where did they go from here?

"Darius, what happens now? I'm not demanding commitment," she added hastily, as he sat back in his chair with an unfathomable expression. Jenny touched his hand. "I know you don't want that."

"Do you," he drawled, his dark eyes half closed. Then, to her consternation, Darius jumped up and her heart tripped with the fear that he was leaving her. She flushed when he dropped to his knees in front of the whole restaurant and held his arms out dramatically. This was so not Darius! "Take me, I'm yours, I can't take it anymore. Do what you will with me, make me your prisoner."

"Darius!" she hissed, her face bright red by now. "Get up."

He didn't, instead to her increasing embarrassment, and the growing amusement around them, Darius shuffled forward on his knees until he was leaning against her lap. "What are you waiting for?" he whispered softly, his eyes gleaming with love and laughter. "This is my final offer, my only offer."

"Oh, go on, put him out of his misery," someone called out, with an amused chuckle.

Jenny's lips parted in a tremulous smile, and she cupped his face in her hands, planting a soft moist kiss on his open mouth.

"If you don't have him, I will," a woman tittered.

"I had better snap you up then, hadn't I," Jenny said, feeling a bubble of happiness rising.

"Darn," another girl giggled. "Just my luck."

Darius's haste was almost indecent, the way he propelled her up to his room, leaving a wave of conversation and laughter behind them.

Darius dispensed with the preliminaries and holding her close with one arm began to unbutton her dress, his mouth forcing hers open in a long, drugging kiss. Her hands were equally as busy, tugging at his shirt. They fell on the bed as one unit, joined before they had even reached it. His violent climax followed shortly after her own explosion of emotion, and they fell apart gasping with exhaustion. He still held her loosely and she could feel his strong heartbeat thudding against her body as he lay beside her.

"Well, that beats a few records," he groaned and laughed ruefully. "I wanted to pleasure you, take my time, but whatever it is you do to me, the effect is so devastating that my body takes over my mind. I said you were a witch, didn't I?" He rolled over onto her again, making her draw her breath in at his obvious readiness. "Let me show you what it should be like," Darius said throatily, as his hands began a mind shattering exploration of her body.

When they finally fell asleep, it was in the early hours of the morning, with the result that they slept right through until the sun sank from sight and the rising moon took its place.

Chapter Twenty-One

Jenny woke up again wondering where she was, then became aware of the long length of masculine body she was resting against. Moonlight streaming through the open curtains fell across Darius, exposing him to her gaze. He was sleeping deeply, his breathing even and soft. She moved gently, trying not to disturb him and raised herself over him, tracing the outline of his chiselled features with her eyes. His thick black lashes rested against his high boned cheeks, hiding his piercing dark eyes. Those same eyes that sparked with such desire when he looked at her.

She followed the line of his broad shoulders, down the powerfully muscled arms that could hold her with such tenderness, one still laying relaxed around her, and on to the hair on his chest which travelled in a broad vee, tapering down to his navel and beyond. The sheet was resting low-down on his hips, partially covering the rest of his body and one long sturdy leg was hanging off the side of the bed.

Jenny was aware, as she observed the raised mound under the sheet covering his loins, that a small movement on her part would uncover the rest of him, and she blushed at her own erotic thoughts. She had never been so uninhibited in her life as she had been with this man, yet could not regret one moment of it. Jenny let her hand rest lightly on his chest, feeling the strong thud of his heart vibrate through her caressing fingers, and she caught her breath at the emotion that flooded her body.

She could not remember ever experiencing anything like this before, such an awesome depth of feeling, as though he were part of her and that she would die if ever it were removed. She had only ever once felt anything near this emotion and Jenny had been a young and impressionable teenager at the time, prone to deep infatuations for unobtainable idols. Then she had met a young boy who had resembled one of her pin ups and had lost her heart and her brains at the same time. No amount of cautioning words or advice could change her mind. He was, Jenny had thought, her soul mate. The be all and end all of her existence, and she had thought that she would die of a broken heart when he had suddenly transferred his affections to another more amenable girlfriend.

Jenny realised now, of course, that the feelings she had experienced then, although so consuming at the time, paled into insignificance compared to how she felt about Darius. This was an adult and very painful love, which had far more impact on her emotions and her life. She gazed down at him, her heart in her eyes, loving him. The way he looked in sleep, strong, yet defenceless. She knew now how much Darius loved her, he had told her so, over and over again as he had made love to her, his voice breaking with passion and emotion. Her heart swelled with an even stronger surge of love at the remembrance of his face dark with desire, his almost desperate lovemaking as though Darius was afraid that Jenny was a dream that would evaporate with the return of daylight, and as if he could sense her thoughts in his sleep, his arms tightened around her pulling her closer. She allowed him to clasp her firmly to him, breathing in his masculine scent and letting the security of his embrace lull her back into a deep sleep.

ɯ ɯ ɯ ɯ ɯ ɯ

Jenny stirred and yawned, stretching tiredly, then groaned as she felt the bruised tenderness in her body. She sat up and leaned carefully over Darius, but he appeared to be still asleep. I should think so, Jenny smirked, he had been insatiable, as her bruises could testify.

"Shall I order some food?" she said softly in his ear, as she became aware that she was hungry. She was taken by surprise when his arm slid around her and rolled her over on top of him.

"I'm hungry, but not for food," Darius growled.

Some while later she surfaced again and glanced furtively at him. This time he was awake and watching her, his face alight with such love that her heart skipped a beat. A slow sensuous smile curved his mouth, as he saw the emotion in her eyes, a look Darius knew was reflected in his own.

"We really do have to eat something, you know," Jenny whispered, as she stroked his chest. "We must sustain your strength if you're going to keep this sort of thing up."

He leaned over, laughing down at her, planting a hard kiss on her lips and groaning as it threatened to develop into something more erotic. With an effort, Darius pulled back, restraining himself. "You're quite right, of course, I can feel even my awesome stamina draining away. Let's eat."

"Stop boasting." Jenny smacked his arm playfully. She laughed as she slid out of his arms and stood up, wrapping her robe around her naked body, aware of the way that his eyes were lingering on her curves and pleaded, "Will you please stop looking at me like that?"

"Like what?" Darius inquired innocently, his eyes wandering appreciatively over her. Jenny threw him an admonishing look and laughing, made her escape into the sitting room, and picked the phone up. As she ordered room service, Darius appeared in the bedroom doorway without a stitch on. She ordered her brain to concentrate on what she was doing, which was very difficult as he began to move menacingly towards her.

"What would you like to eat?" she asked in a strangled voice.

"You," Darius mouthed.

Jenny blushed and put her hand over the mouthpiece, as though he could be heard. Darius laughed throatily at her pink face and continued his advance, and she put the phone down with a shaky laugh. It seemed that food would have to wait.

ൡ ൡ ൡ ൡ ൡ ൡ

While Darius lay half dozing in the bed, Jenny took the opportunity to grab a shower. As she reached for the soap, the bathroom door opened, making her jump, and the bar shot from out of her fingers landing beneath Darius's foot as he walked forward. As his feet slid from beneath him, he went down with a painful thud, letting loose a muffled oath.

"Are you hurt?" Jenny asked anxiously, as she rushed over to him.

Darius had been holding his breath. Now he let it out in a rush as he rubbed his hip. "Bruised, I think. I see that you're practicing your trade again."

"Trade?" She blinked in puzzlement.

"Witchcraft, you maddening woman," he laughed.

Jenny leaned over Darius, making him very aware of her warm pink naked body, as she massaged the tender spot on his side. He groaned loudly, and she looked down at him worriedly. "What is it, am I hurting you?"

"No," Darius answered huskily, his eyes gleaming darkly at her, and a faint smile on his lips.

"Ah!" Jenny smirked, as she moved over him. "I can sense a growing problem between us."

"That's funny, I can feel it too," Darius grinned wickedly, as he pulled her down to meet his mouth. As his lips released hers, he slid her against his body, positioning her expertly and causing Jenny to gasp with shock.

"That was skilfully done," she giggled against his chest.

"I did it for you," Darius said, his voice slightly uneven. "We have now tucked the growing problem out of sight."

Then his breath caught in a hoarse groan as she moved against him and all laughter vanished as emotion wrapped an ever-tightening band around them, securing them in dark primal space, making his body respond urgently to hers.

As they lay recovering, Darius propped himself up on one elbow and gazed down at her lovingly, tenderly stroking the curls back off her forehead. "I love your hair, do you know that? I think I wanted to grab handfuls of it the first time I saw you."

"You mean you wanted to tear it out?" Jenny laughed up at him.

"Maybe, at first, then I wanted you with a depth of feeling that frightened me. I didn't want that sort of involvement." His face became serious, as Darius felt her slight withdrawal. He held her face between his large, strong hands, giving it a slight squeeze. "Past tense, I want you, need you, love you desperately. Don't break my heart and tell me that you don't feel the same. One more thing, and let me make this crystal clear, I assure you that there is absolutely nothing going on between Melissa and I, never was, so dismiss her from your mind. If something goes wrong and you leave me again, you might as well tear my heart out and take it with you. I can't function without knowing that you're mine."

As he looked down at her, Darius suddenly felt helpless at the power this small, fragile woman wielded over him. Darius loved her so much that he found it hard to imagine how he had existed without her. He could not stand to think that maybe her feelings were not as deeply entrenched as his own. He stared down into her large green eyes searchingly with a slight smile on his face, but Jenny could see the anxiety in his eyes, and she couldn't bear it, so she tried to put his mind at rest.

"You know very well that I love you. I think I loved you the first moment you threw your naked body onto mine," she said, gazing up at him mischievously as he laughed.

"You dreadful woman, so you only want me for my body? Well, I'm sure that can be remedied." He let his hand caress her throat. "What do you think now; is my intellect a bit higher than a slug's, and how about my personality, does it rank better than a bug's?"

"Oh, that rankled, did it?" Jenny laughed softly, as she took his hand and touched his fingers to her mouth, then bit them gently.

"If you don't stop doing that, we could end up here for another day, which would give me time to nibble you all over," Darius said softly.

"Promise?" she breathed, closing her eyes as he lowered his head.

"I always keep my promises," he purred. His voice trailed away, as his eyes dwelt on her lips, and Darius gave in weakly to the invitation that beckoned.

רורוו ורורו

"Come on, let's get packed, go home and tell the family that you've caught me at last," Darius said lazily a few hours later when they surfaced. "Let's put them all out of their misery."

"Misery?" Jenny looked up at him questioningly.

"Yes, apparently I have been acting like some obnoxious overbearing Jekyll and Hyde character." He smiled tenderly at her and pressed his finger to her lips, laughing as she went to agree. "They'll be relieved to see me back to normal at last."

"I'm sure they will, Darius." Jenny hid a smile, as she thought of his usual arrogant bearing. He cast her a suspicious look, but she scattered any coherent thoughts from his mind by twining herself around him. His last thought before Darius sank, was that his life would never be the same again. The Witchfinder General could go back into retirement; he was no longer needed. If Jenny was a witch, then he was her willing victim.

About the Author

Essa Sims lives in England near the sea. A lifelong lover of painting and reading, she turned to writing as her family gained independence, allowing her to fully embrace her passions.

Romance captivates her the most, and her stories feature rugged heroes and strong-willed heroines whose fiery clashes create exciting, racy interactions. With humour skilfully woven into their lively banter, Essa writes delightful tales that keep readers eagerly turning the pages.

www.ingramcontent.com/pod-product-compliance
Ingram Content Group UK Ltd.
Pitfield, Milton Keynes, MK11 3LW, UK
UKHW040134260225
455541UK00001B/51

9 798230 547679